# THE CONFEDERATION
# OF THE PEOPLE

HARLAN HAGUE

WOLFPACK
PUBLISHING
— EST 2013 —

**WOLFPACK PUBLISHING**
— EST 2013 —

The Confederation of The People
Paperback Edition
Copyright © 2021 (As Revised) Harlan Hague

Wolfpack Publishing
6032 Wheat Penny Avenue
Las Vegas, NV 89122

ISBN: 978-1-64734-076-6 (paperback) 978-1-64734-075-9 (ebook)

# THE CONFEDERATION
# OF THE PEOPLE

# CHAPTER ONE

## Who the Hell Are We Fighting?

The silence was absolute. Except for the distant cascading trill of a canyon wren, which repeated once and ended.

Sheer sandstone canyon walls in subdued hues of crimson, vermillion, gold and tan looked down on a sand valley with scattered patches of green grass. A shallow stream of powder blue water meandered between low banks. Clusters of willows and occasional cottonwoods grew at the water's edge. Wildflowers colored the flat near the stream and the gentle slope above it. There were tiny pink buttercups and the little bell-like flowers of the yellow fritillary. The delicate, sweet scent of yellow biscuitroot was pervasive. The appearance of all announced the end of winter.

A light breeze raised a swirling cloud of sand on the stream bank, settled, and it was still again. The silver gray sky was clear, not a cloud in sight. On this early spring day, the midday sun was warm, not yet hot. When spring gave way to summer, then it would be hot. Well before midday.

The dwelling was small, enough for a family and a parent or two. It was circular, with a wall of dried mud and tree bark tamped between and over vertical poles. The round wall slanted gently inward toward a conical roof. A doorway framed with cottonwood poles faced eastward to catch the morning sun and its good blessings. A colorful blanket hung limply from the lintel.

The home looked very much like a hogan, though the land of the Navajo was far southward. A neat garden lay near the dwelling. The healthy young green plants, corn, squash and beans, promised a bountiful harvest. Beyond the garden, the branches of a small peach orchard were covered with tight buds and a few scattered light pink early blossoms.

Then it began. Soft clinking and creaking sounds intruded on the silence. The sounds gradually increased and became the metallic clatter of bridle hardware and creak of saddle leather, accompanied by the sounds of hooves on hard ground. The sounds increased gradually as the animals moved closer.

A party of thirty mounted United States Army troopers with four packhorses rode over a rising and flowed down the embankment. They walked their horses toward the hogan. The troop reined in and stopped in front of the dwelling. Two soldiers dismounted. They handed their reins to comrades and pulled rifles from saddle buckets. They stood a moment by their mounts, watching the hogan. They walked slowly to the door, carrying their rifles at the ready. The lead soldier brushed the hanging blanket aside carefully with the barrel of his rifle, stooped and went inside.

After a moment, the soldier came out and shook his head. He leaned casually against the side of the hogan, his rifle cradled loosely in the crook of his arm. His partner took the reins of their horses and tied them to a scrub cedar beside the dwelling.

The other soldiers rode over the garden toward the orchard. When they had passed, the garden was gone. Only bits of shredded green leaves remained, crushed into the soft soil by the horses' hooves.

The troopers reined in at the edge of the orchard. They dismounted and tied their reins to tree limbs. About half of the force removed rifles from saddle buckets and casually took up defensive positions near the horses. Some faced the valley beyond the dwelling. Others looked toward the hillside above the orchard.

A half dozen troopers walked to the packhorses. They untied knots and pulled axes from the packs. Hefting the axes, they walked toward the peach trees. The first soldier to reach a tree stopped beside the trunk. He spread his legs and leaned the ax handle against his thigh, braced himself and spit on his hands. He lifted the ax and swung it hard in a wide loop toward the trunk. The blade bit into live wood with a loud thunk.

There was an immediate whistling sound followed by a loud explosion among the tethered horses. Another burst erupted near the bunched-up soldiers who faced the hillside. Horses and troopers were blown off their feet, lacerated and bloody. Horses jerked on their reins, and some of the leather traces broke. The freed mounts galloped down the slope toward the stream.

Soldiers on guard looked around frantically for the source of the explosions. The troopers at the trees dropped the axes and ran to their terrified horses where they pulled rifles from buckets. They formed a ragged defensive circle. Against what? They saw no enemy.

Another whistling sound rent the air, and there was another explosion that just missed the bunched-up soldiers.

They looked around in confusion. The troopers ran to their horses, thrust rifles into buckets and untied reins with shaking hands. The horses stomped and shied sideways as the troopers tried to mount. Two soldiers had the reins pulled from their grasp, and their horses galloped down the hill, followed by two packhorses. Contents of the open packs bounced out and scattered.

The other troopers mounted with difficulty, pulling up behind them soldiers whose horses had bolted or been killed. The soldiers galloped in disarray up the trail toward the rising from whence they had come. The two troopers at the back held the leads of packhorses that scattered the contents of their open packs in the wake of the retreating patrol.

A lone Indian stepped from behind an outcropping. He was dressed only in breechclout and moccasins. He braced himself, raised a tubular apparatus to his shoulder and pointed it at the departing troopers. He fired. The projectile hit the ground behind the galloping horses and exploded, sending up sprays of sand and rock.

The warrior lowered the weapon. He watched as the dust cloud raised by the fleeing troopers rose, thinned and vanished in the light breeze as the horsemen rode over the rising and disappeared. The sounds of the galloping horses diminished and died.

It was quiet again. A wren's call broke the silence, perhaps the same that had sung before. It was farther away this time.

The Indian looked in the direction of the wren's call. He listened a moment, turned and walked around the outcropping behind him. He stopped beside two warriors who squatted on the ground beside small mortars. They looked up at him and smiled. A pyramid of projectiles lay on the ground beside each mortar.

Beyond the mortars, twenty warriors sat on a gentle slope, looking intently at the shooter. Most wore only breechclout and moccasins. Some also wore hide leggings. Each man held a rifle across his lap.

The tufted hairgrass was knee-high. It rippled like green ocean waves in the light breeze. Blue and pink penstemon and purple fireweed poked their heads above the swaying grass.

The land of the wide valley rolled in gentle contours between the distant ranges of hills on the two sides. A narrow stream of sky blue water, hardly three feet wide and six inches deep, flowed down the center of the expanse.

A neat one-room cabin of freshly hewn logs lay near the stream. The only other structure was a small log building that doubled as an outhouse and stable. A single plowed furrow ran from the stream toward the cabin.

A wagon with two stout mules in harness stood before the cabin. A man in his thirties, a woman about the same age, and two children, a boy age seven and a girl of five, sat on the wagon seat. The woman held the little girl close with both of her arms, tears streaming down the girl's face. The boy was stiffly defiant. The wagon was piled with furniture, bedding, clothing, tools, a plow, all they owned.

Five Indians stood near the wagon, rifles cradled in their arms. Their dress identified them as Beothuk.

The man held the lines of the team. He glared at the Beothuk. He wore dirty overalls and a faded blue shirt that was stained and wet with his fear. He was scared, but he was also angry.

"I'll be back," he said. "This is my land."

Howahkan stepped over to stand beside the team. He

looked up at the farmer. The Indian's face betrayed no anger, rather pity. And understanding. He was not a big man, but he was muscular and hard. Only his face revealed the hardships of his sixty years.

Howahkan replied calmly in English. "This is not your land. This is not your country. Go. Find a good place for your children." He poked the near mule with his rifle barrel. The mule jerked.

The settler flinched. He glared at Howahkan. His wife gripped his arm. She wore the apron and simple homemade cotton dress that she wore when the Beothuk rode into their yard. Tears streaked her cheeks.

She pulled gently on his arm. "Please, David," she said softly.

The settler looked at her a long moment, then turned to glare again at Howahkan, choking back his own tears as he felt his dreams slipping away. He jerked back to the front and roughly shook the team's lines. The mules strained in their harness, and the wagon lurched and moved forward.

The settlers' cabin burned furiously. Flames licked up the wall and rose from the timber and moss roof. The five Beothuk stood nearby, watching the fire. The roof collapsed, and a huge red and orange ball of fire rolled upward from the center of the cabin. The Beothuk jumped backward in surprise. They laughed, gesturing at the fiery spectacle. All but Howahkan.

The five turned and walked toward their horses nearby where they were tied to the low branches of a scrub pine. They stopped. They looked toward the low hillside where the settler's wagon had disappeared, listening to the faint rumble of galloping animals.

"Buffalo?" said one. They listened, frozen.

"No!" Howahkan said.

They ran toward their horses. The galloping sounds grew louder as the Indians frantically untied their reins.

A troop of horsemen burst over the crest of the low hill and flowed down the near slope. They were United States Army troopers, a patrol of twenty soldiers. As they galloped hard toward the Indians, the troopers opened fire with rifles and pistols.

Two warriors were immediately hit and fell. Howahkan mounted hurriedly, pulled his rifle from its case and fired on the troopers. The two other Indians tried to mount, but their terrified horses reared, pulled their reins from their grasp and galloped away.

One of the Indians slapped Howahkan's horse on the flank. The horse shied and galloped up the slope behind the burning cabin. Howahkan drummed the sides of the horse with his heels.

The charging troopers were within thirty yards. They dropped rifles into saddle buckets and drew their sabers. As they closed on the Indians, they lowered the tips.

The two remaining Indians pulled small iron balls from their belts and threw them toward the charging soldiers. The balls fell in front of the galloping horses and rolled. The missiles exploded as the horses passed over them, killing two horses and their riders. The other horses shied violently sideways, throwing some riders.

Other troopers rode the two warriors down, killing them with saber thrusts.

First light. A force of fifty soldiers quietly sat their horses in the deep shade at the edge of a wood. They looked down a grassy slope at a small Beothuk village in a flat, about two hundred yards distant. The green slope was lightly colored with scattered white camas flowers and tall bastard toadflax with its clusters of tiny pink and white flowers.

Twenty tipis were scattered along the banks of a shallow stream that ran at the back of the village. Across the stream, a small herd of horses grazed on the lush fescue grasses on the bottom. There were grays, whites, roans and paints in a multitude of colors. Each was tethered by a rawhide line tied above the hoof and secured to a stake.

Four women and three men stood at a cooking fire in front of a tipi. Behind them, and beside almost every tipi, racks were heavy with strips of meat, drying in the warm sun. The air was still, and the smoke from the fires rose in thin, transparent columns.

The Indians looked directly at the soldiers. A woman bent down to stir something in a metal pot. Another picked up a short piece of dry limb and placed it on the fire. No weapons were in sight.

Lieutenant Worth sat his horse at the edge of the wood. He looked at every detail of the village and its surroundings, left to right and back again. He studied the terrain from the patrol's position down the slope to the village. He squeezed his knees slightly, and his mount walked slowly from the wood into the open.

At thirty-five, Lieutenant Worth was the oldest lieutenant in the command, but he was respected as one of its most capable officers. He had risen through the ranks and had won his commission in battle. He was sufficiently confident that he was neither offended nor angered when someone observed that he had not attended West Point. In fact, it was usually he who broke in the green West Pointers when they arrived at their new posting.

He turned his head slightly to the side and spoke softly. "All right, sergeant." Sergeant Clark rode from the wood up behind Lieutenant Worth. Clark turned his horse around to face the wood.

He spoke sharply. "Form up! Boot-to-boot!" Sergeant Clark was a model soldier. He had joined the army at eighteen and had served honorably in the frontier army for twenty-two years. He was competent and reliable. He was content.

Troopers walked their horses from the wood in good order. They formed a single line, boot-to-boot. Sergeant Clark wheeled his horse and faced front. The bugler rode up beside Clark. He held the reins in his right hand, his bugle in his left.

"Sir!" said Sergeant Clark.

The line of horses undulated and reformed smartly, waved and reformed again. The only sounds were the wind in the prairie grasses and the clinking of bridle fittings and the creak of saddles.

Lieutenant Worth drew his saber and came to the carry, with the guard at his right hip and the blade against the shoulder. Still looking forward, he shouted: "Draw sabers!"

Sergeant Clark and the troopers drew their sabers and came to the carry. The blades sparkled and waved gently as the horses shifted from side to side.

"Bugler, sound Forward March," said Lieutenant Worth. The bugler raised the horn to his lips and blew Forward March. The line of troopers walked their horses forward in tight formation, boot-to-boot. Lieutenant Worth was followed by Sergeant Clark and the bugler, followed by the line of troopers.

After twenty paces, the bugler sounded Trot March. The troopers urged their mounts into a trot and raised their sabers aloft. The riders maintained boot-to-boot order, but the line was more ragged now, undulating and reforming, undulating and reforming.

After an additional sixty paces, the bugler sounded Gallop March. Lieutenant Worth and the soldiers kicked their mounts into a gallop, trying to stay in tight formation.

After an additional eighty paces, the bugler blew Charge.

Lieutenant Worth lowered the tip of his saber and pointed it forward. The line of troopers swept down the slope toward the village. The line widened slightly, but still maintained a rough boot-to-boot formation.

The Indians saw them coming. For a moment, they did nothing, as if the charging mass had no meaning for them, as if they were merely onlookers. Then the three men walked casually toward the tipis. The four women abandoned their cooking and ran toward the stream. They waded the shallow flow and tried to settle the restless horses.

No other people were visible in the village.

As the cavalry bore down on the outskirts of the village, their charge was impeded by large stones and heavy brush that forced the troopers into two wide funnels. Not by chance.

In the path of the galloping horses in each of the two funnels, a long line of spears sprang from the earth, throwing off the grasses that had hidden them. The stout spears, spaced two feet apart in a horizontal frame, were metal, six feet long. With their butt ends anchored in the ground, they pointed toward the charging horses at a forty-five-degree angle.

Troopers shouted in surprise and pulled back hard on their reins. Some horses slid, fell to the ground and rolled dangerously close to the spears. Other horses could not stop quickly enough and were impaled. Some riders were thrown from their horses and were propelled onto the spear points. The lucky ones who were thrown fell below the spear points, clambered up and ran for cover. The injured could only cry for help.

Simultaneously with the release of the spears, about thirty warriors burst from tipis, carrying rifles. They shouldered their weapons and fired again and again on the troopers. Their shots hit soldiers who had been thrown from their horses and others, still mounted, who milled around near the spear points.

Mounted troopers pulled their unhorsed comrades up behind them and rode away at a gallop. Some were shot down as they fled. The survivors rode up the slope into the wood from whence they began the action.

The villagers walked to the line of spears and surveyed the carnage. The army had left fourteen dead at the spear line and four more on the slope. There were no Indian casualties.

The army bivouac was set up in a meadow bordered by low hills that sloped gently upward from the flat. A small spring at the bottom of the camp bubbled from the ground and flowed lazily in a narrow, shallow stream.

The grassy terrain between the camp and the crest of the hills was mostly open with little cover behind which a hostile could hide. Two-man tents were pitched on each side of an open lane. In the darkness, soldiers sat around small campfires for warmth and light, eating their usual beans, salt pork and hardtack from metal plates. There was little conversation. Most were somber, content to eat in silence and contemplation. On the other hand, a few soldiers chattered, cracked jokes and grinned with kindred spirits. These last had taken no part in the day's combat.

At the end of the line of tents, Lieutenant Worth and Lieutenant Michael Wagner leaned against a wagon. Lieutenant Wagner was a handsome twenty-three-year-old, hard and trim. He was well trained, confident and eager. He had arrived at his first frontier posting only a few days before this first patrol. It was a literal baptism by fire, though he had not taken part in the attack on the village. Lieutenant Worth had left him to secure the bivouac.

"I never saw anything like it," Worth said. "I've seen them use wooden spears, like willow, but these spears were machined metal. And the setup had springs. I know. I got a close look. My horse slid and spun, and I was thrown off. Right between two shafts. I was damn lucky."

Lieutenant Wagner frowned. "What about the rifles? You're sure they fired more than once without reloading?"

Lieutenant Worth nodded sharply. "Yes. I'm sure of it."

"Mmm." Wagner pondered. "I heard at the Point that they were working on a repeater, but they said it would be years before the Army got them."

"The damned savages have repeating rifles," said Worth, "and we're stuck with a single-shot breech-loading carbine and a single-shot muzzle-loading percussion pistol. Damn! What other surprises have they got for us?"

His question was answered from the sky. The bivouac was light as day. The lieutenants looked up. They saw a brilliant flare high in the sky that illuminated the camp. Soldiers jumped up. They stared at the flare, dumbfounded, and squinted at its brilliance. They looked around at the camp. Everything was as clearly defined as in daylight.

Their attention was diverted by a new threat. From the darkness on the hillside above the camp, flaming arrows shot high into the air. The arrows described a slow arc and fell into the campground. Tents and wagons burst into flame. Sharp cries came from soldiers who were hit.

Troopers recovered. They ran to tents and grabbed their rifles. The soldiers aimed toward the source of the arrows. They lowered the rifles. All they saw was darkness.

They looked up at the light. The flare dimmed, drifted slowly downward and burned out. The camp was dark again, but for the campfires and burning tents and wagons.

Lieutenant Worth looked at the smoldering bivouac. "What in hell is going on? Who the hell are we fighting?"

The sun ball lay on the eastern horizon. Tents were down and the three wagons packed. Mule teams were hitched and shifted idly in their harness. Troopers sat their horses in two columns of two. On Sergeant Clark's command, his detachment of thirty men fell in behind him and rode down alongside the stream. They were bound for the site of yesterday's battle where they would recover the bodies of their comrades.

The other force moved off behind Lieutenants Worth and Wagner. Teamsters shook their lines and pulled their wagons into place at the end of the column. The formation rode up and over a low embankment and disappeared from view.

A warrior who had been hidden high above the camp behind a dense cluster of bush hawthorn stood. He stared across the flat at the embankment where the column had vanished. Satisfied that the soldiers had indeed gone, he walked to the top of the slope and down the opposite side.

The warrior bent and picked up a rawhide bag. He loosed the leather thongs at the top and took out two short wooden staffs with small white canvas flags attached at the end. He looked toward a hill in the distance. He raised the two signal flags vertically over his head, then lowered them to a horizontal position on each side of his body, then dropped them down to his sides.

He waited. On the distant hill, a figure returned the same signal. The warrior then proceeded to send his message. He waved the two flags up, down, out, sending a message by semaphore. At the end, he dropped his arms to his sides.

The Indian in the distance returned a signal: his right arm at 135 degrees, his left arm at 45 degrees, then reversed the position: left arm at 135 degrees, right arm at 45 degrees, then down to his sides. Received and understood. This warrior then turned around and began signaling to still another compatriot on a distant hilltop.

# CHAPTER TWO

## Fort Andrew Jackson and the Golden Goose

Fort Andrew Jackson was only three years old, but it had already proven its worth. The region was peaceful for the most part, and the army was content to improve the fort's amenities and endure the typical boredom of frontier post life.

Visitors to the fort were surprised that it had achieved high efficiency in such a short time. The beginnings of the fort were a bit different from the usual. So far as possible, the soldiers assigned to the fort had been chosen as much for their background as their military capabilities.

Troopers had been handpicked from among the ranks and recruits who had some experience in the building trades. There were precious few who satisfied this requirement, but an occasional frontier farm boy had helped his pa build a log house, or a city boy had worked as a carpenter's apprentice. Upon arriving at their new prairie post, the troopers were put to work at construction. Six months from the turning of the first spade on the first foundation, the fort was finished and fully functioning.

It appeared that the fort was built on a flat, but closer inspection revealed a gentle slope from the top to the river at the bottom. The layout of the fort was open, with buildings grouped around a spacious parade ground of fescue bunch grass. In the center of the parade, atop a tall flagpole, the stars and stripes hung limply in the still air.

The top, the south side of the parade, was officers' country. The commander's house was an imposing frame building with dormer windows and a covered porch. Quarters for officers were located on each side of the commander's house. For married officers, there were a few single-family dwellings and others that housed two families each. Single officers shared a couple of these units. These lucky few checked the roster of incoming officers often since they knew they would have to give up the choice units if married officers arrived at the post.

Most bachelor officers were quartered in a long frame building that was notorious for its parties. Birthday parties, victory celebrations, parties to break the monotony of waiting. The hospital lay beside the bachelor officers' quarters, the better to accommodate the casualties of revelry, some said.

Across the parade, on the north side, there were the mess halls and four long barracks that housed the troopers of the six mounted companies, a little over three hundred soldiers total. This was far under the allotted numbers, a usual problem for the frontier army.

Adjacent to the mess halls lay the wonder of the fort and the delight of all, the icehouse. Mostly underground, the well-insulated structure was filled with blocks of ice cut from the frozen river in winter. With careful management, the supply would last through the summer. The supply was always sufficient for officers' drinks.

The laundries and quarters of the laundresses were

nearby. Some of the laundresses were married to enlisted men. A persistent rumor suggested that some of the single women augmented their meager pay by providing other sundry services to the soldiers.

At some distance beyond the barracks, horses and cattle grazed on the lush grassy bottom. Spacious corrals and stables built of logs and planks provided support for the seven or eight hundred mounts and draft animals. Cattle corrals lay nearby. Adjacent in the bottom, the large post garden was walled to keep out the fort's animals.

A short distance east of the corrals along the river, the post cemetery was laid out. Until two days ago, there had been but five graves. Two laundresses and three soldiers who had been members of an ambushed woodcutting party were buried there. New graves marked by bare mounded earth held the bodies of those killed in recent actions.

On the east side of the parade, a long adobe and stone structure housed the sutler's store and a large room at the back that might serve for a meeting or a band concert. The sutler's store was a trading post, offering goods that might interest soldiers, settlers or the occasional Indian visitor. The sutler assured his customers that if he did not have something they wanted, he could order it from back east. Payment in advance. The sutler was not military. He conducted his business under a license from the War Department.

Behind the store, two warehouses contained supplies for the post's mess halls and all the other detritus required by a large military establishment. Beyond the warehouses, toward the river, lay two solid stone buildings, the guardhouse and the magazine.

No walls encircled the post. Forts throughout history, including those east of the Mississippi River, had been protected from their enemies by strong walls. But military planners had decided that they wanted to project an image of strength in the West, that the army need not cower behind walls for protection, that they were strong and in control. Thus, no walls.

Located in a region of fertile valleys and plains and near a substantial stream, the fort was expected to protect settlers that were moving closer to the region. The fly in the ointment was the Indians who had hunted, gathered and lived in these same valleys and mountains for centuries.

Major Edmund Burke, the fort commandant, was aware of the task ahead of him. The peace that he and his soldiers enjoyed was in direct proportion to the absence of settlers. This was about to change.

A few hundred miles east of the fort, a farmer might be able to buy goods at a general store within a day's ride. If he were fortunate, he might be able to visit a neighbor only an hour's ride away. Not all people who lived on the frontier were of like mind. Some began to fret when they could see the smoke from their closest neighbor's chimney. The solution was to move west where there were great expanses of empty land, theirs for the taking.

Major Burke, Captain Jackson, Lieutenant Worth and Lieutenant Wagner sat in rocking chairs in a semi-circle before a crackling fire in the fireplace at the commandant's house. Burke often convened a gathering of officers at his quarters. He favored the informal atmosphere of a sitting room to the sterile post offices. Later, when the early spring tempests had moderated, he would hold forth on his covered porch.

A laid-back career officer in his late fifties, Major Burke had a reputation for fairness and a calm demeanor. Not to say that he was soft. He could speak gently to a subordinate soldier in one breath and order him flogged in the next. The difference between him and many of his peers was that the soldier would deserve the flogging.

Captain Jackson was second in command at the fort. He was a do-it-by-the book West Pointer. A reliable, uninspired plodder. He was pleased to be asked whether he was kin to the fort's namesake. He patiently replied that he was not, though relishing the shared name.

The four officers stared at the dancing flames and sipped from the glasses they held. The major was relentless in his efforts to prevent drunkenness in the ranks. He often placed severe restrictions on traders to limit the flow of alcohol to the soldiers. But he was fond of his spirits and had an ample supply of whiskey for his guests.

Lieutenant Worth drank from his glass. "These savages have weapons we've never even heard of," he said.

"They're certainly not getting them from our traders," Captain Jackson said, "and the British don't have them. So where are they getting them?"

Major Burke leaned forward and stared at the windows on the front of the sitting room. He moved from side to side in his chair to catch a glimpse through the windows. "Maybe I'll ask them," he said.

The other three officers turned and followed his gaze. Burke stood and walked to the front door, opened it and walked outside to the porch. He turned to look back inside. "Come here," he said. The others stood and walked outside to stand with him on the porch.

They saw a group of Indians, four men and one woman, striding across the parade. The Indians were dressed in traditional Beothuk skin clothing, quilled, beaded and fringed. They apparently knew where they were going and were anxious to get there. They looked neither right nor left.

"I'm meeting them later today," Major Burke said. "They want to talk."

"What do they want to talk about?" Worth said.

"We'll see," Burke said.

"Do they speak for The People?" Lieutenant Wagner said.

Major Burke frowned. "You've been here, what, five days? What do you know about The People?"

"I understand it's a confederation of some sort," Wagner said, "mostly the Plains tribes, but with some communication with other tribes."

The officers watched the Indians as they passed in front of the sutler's store and disappeared behind the building.

Major Burke walked back inside, and the others followed. They sat down and retrieved their glasses. Burke picked up the whiskey bottle and walked around, refreshing their drinks. He sat, raised his glass and emptied it.

"It's more than communication," Burke said. "It's cooperation. It seems the confederation includes tribes from hundreds of miles from here. I received a message just this morning that told about the progress of the southern command that is under orders to clear a particularly attractive river valley of Utes so it can be opened for settlement. Or lack of progress, I should say. The Utes seem to have the same sort of ordnance that the Beothuk have.

"It's damned unexpected, this confederation. Tribes have been fighting each other for centuries. Now they seem to agree that they have an enemy more dangerous than the tribe over the hill."

"Makes sense," Wagner said. The major looked at him and raised an eyebrow. "Logical, I mean, from their point of view."

"Yeah. Logical. Too damned logical. Makes our job harder," said Burke. The four leaned back in their chairs and rocked slowly, staring into the fire. They sipped their drinks.

Jackson turned to Wagner. "Do you know what they call us?" Wagner shook his head. "Wasichus," Jackson said, "the fat takers, the greedy people, people that want it all."

Major Burke leaned forward and set his empty glass on the table. He stood and hitched up his trousers. He stepped to the fireplace and warmed his hands. He turned around to face the three officers.

"Names are not important," Burke said. "What is important is where in hell are they getting the stuff? We must find the golden goose. And kill it."

# CHAPTER THREE

## Ambassador to The People

At first glance, the sutler's store looked like any general store anywhere in the country. There were kitchen utensils, needles and pins, tobacco and cigars, candy, ready-to-wear clothes, hats, yard goods, tea, sardines, dried fish and buttons, virtually anything that was not considered sufficiently necessary by the army to have it stocked in army stores.

No alcoholic beverages. A sutler could lose his license.

Then one might notice the local products, like finely dressed animal skins, rawhide purses and beaded vests. Lieutenant Wagner picked up a small pouch made of soft deerskin from a display table. The pouch was decorated with quills and tiny colored glass beads. He liked it, but knew that he had no use for it. He replaced it on the table and looked up.

And saw her. She stood across the room, looking at some cooking utensils. She held a small iron frying pan, turning it back and forth, examining it. Wagner stared. He had seen many Indian women, but not like this girl. She was—how old— nineteen, twenty? He guessed she was about five feet, five inches, with two braids of waist-length black hair that hung over her shoulders in front.

She was stunning, her dark eyes showing the slightest Asian cast. Her skin was light olive, smooth and without a blemish. He could almost feel the softness of her cheeks. She wore a soft, fringed deerskin jacket over a tan cotton dress, richly embroidered in bright colors, and skin leggings. A thin round metal disk was attached to the jacket above her breast. The metal was smooth, colored a subdued blue. A symbol, a hieroglyph of some sort, was etched or engraved on the surface.

A silver necklace with turquoise stones hung around her neck. She wore a second necklace of thin plaited rawhide. A bone pendant hung from the strand. The pendant, about four inches long, appeared to be carved, but Wagner could not make it out. The woman looked up and saw him. She immediately looked down at the pan she held. She replaced it on the table and walked toward the door.

She stopped at the doorway to look at some woolen scarves that hung from pegs on the wall. She touched a scarf, feeling the soft material between her fingers. She turned back and saw that Wagner still stared at her. She released the scarf and walked to the door.

He exhaled.

The room had a floor and walls of rough-hewn planks. It was bare of adornment and furniture but for a rectangular table and ten chairs. Major Burke and Captain Jackson sat at the table. Lieutenants Worth and Wagner sat in chairs on their right, away from the table and near the windows. Major Burke had explained to the two lieutenants that he wanted them to observe the proceedings.

On the other side of the table, two Beothuk men sat in chairs facing Major Burke. One was Howahkan, the same who had led the eviction of the settler and his family. It was obvious from the manner in which the others deferred to him that he was the leader of this delegation.

Howahkan was dressed simply in a hair-fringed buckskin shirt, breechclout and leggings. In his long hair, he wore two coup feathers and around his neck a bear-claw necklace. The others wore traditional clothing, mostly Beothuk with a smattering of styles from other plains tribes. They wore trinkets from local and distant tribes.

Howahkan and the others also were adorned with small metal disks attached to clothing and as pendants around their necks. The disks were similar to that worn by the girl, blue in color and each engraved with a hieroglyphic symbol, though not the same symbol as hers. Howahkan also wore a tarnished silver chain around his neck from which hung a heavy round silver pendant. An image was stamped on the face of the disk, but Wagner couldn't make it out.

Wagner stared past Howahkan to the three Indians who sat in a second row. One was the young woman he had seen in the sutler's store. She looked up and made eye contact, then looked down at her hands in her lap.

Wagner started at Major Burke's voice.

"We are glad to see you here," Burke said. "We will listen to what you say."

Howahkan shifted in his chair. He sat stiffly upright, frowning. "I am Howahkan. I have lived in these valleys and these hills sixty winters. Now wasichus wish to come and live where I live. Why is this? I do not go to live in their country."

"I understand what you say," said Major Burke.

"The Americans scare the buffalo," Howahkan said, "and it is harder for us to hunt them." Howahkan waited, but Burke looked blankly at him. "Some wasichus have built cabins and plowed the earth in the Valley of Plum Trees."

"Yes, I know," Major Burke said. "I understand."

Howahkan waited, but Burke was silent. "Then you will tell them that they must leave this valley?" Howahkan said.

Major Burke held up his hand, palm outward. "No, I cannot do that. The Great White Father in Washington says that these people have a right to that land. No Beothuk live there, and you do not need the land."

Howahkan glared at Major Burke. "Your Great White Father in Washington has no power here! The Great Spirit gave this land to The People to use and pass to our children. The wasichus must leave!"

Major Burke looked at the floor, then at the ceiling. His face betrayed no anger, rather frustration. He turned back to Howahkan. "I hear you, and I understand," Burke said. "We will pay you to give up the valley. We will give you bolts of cloth, blankets, pots and fry pans, skinning knives, tobacco and beads."

Howahkan stiffened and leaned forward, almost rising from his chair in anger. "No! We cannot sell the land. We do not own it. We use it."

Worth and Wagner exchanged glances.

Major Burke leaned back in his chair. He sighed and leaned forward. He placed his arms on the table and clasped his hands. "Howahkan. We want peace. We do not want to fight The People . . . Where do you get the repeating rifles and the exploding weapons?"

Howahkan glared at Major Burke. "You will not tell them to leave?"

Burke leaned back in his chair and looked blankly at Howahkan. Howahkan waited, but the major said no more.

Howahkan stood abruptly and strode toward the door.

The other Beothuk followed. Just before reaching the door, the girl turned and made eye contact with Lieutenant Wagner. Her countenance was soft, questioning.

Major Burke and Lieutenant Wagner sat in rocking chairs before the cold fireplace in the commandant's sitting room. Each held a small glass of whiskey. They stared into the dark fireplace. Wagner still wondered why he was called alone to the commandant's house.

"Two things," Burke said. "We're on the edge of some big trouble. If it breaks before we find out where they're getting the armaments, we may not be able to hold out here."

"Do you think they're finished talking?" Wagner said.

Major Burke took the bottle from the table beside his chair and filled his glass. He stood and proffered the bottle to Wagner.

"No, thank you, sir."

Burke nodded and set the bottle on the table. He walked over to the cold fireplace and held out his hands, as if to warm them. He turned to face Wagner. "That's the other thing," Burke said. "Old Howahkan is not afraid of anything or anybody. But I don't think he wants war. Sometimes he rattles his war gourd, and sometimes he is downright rational. You saw him storm out of here yesterday."

"Yes, sir," Wagner said. "Looks bad." He looked at the ashes in the dark fireplace.

"Yes, except he sent the woman and her interpreter back this morning to ask for someone to be sent to his village. To stay there. The way she describes it, he wants nothing less than a United States ambassador to The People. Can you imagine that?"

Wagner started and looked up at the major. "The woman who was with him yesterday?" He hoped he sounded casual, the opposite of what he felt.

Burke looked back into the fireplace. "Yes."

"Sounds interesting," Wagner said. "Would Washington buy it?"

Burke sat down in his rocker. "I've sent word, with my recommendation that we accept."

"I hope we're here to receive the reply," said Wagner.

"I'm not waiting. I'm sending someone presently. You."

"Me?" Wagner recoiled. He frowned. "I'm no diplomat, sir."

"You'd better be a fast learner. You're recently out of the Point. You left there with high marks and came here with top recommendations. So you'll have friends if Washington decides that we're crazy." Major Burke smiled and drank from his glass. Wagner grimaced and looked into the dark fireplace.

"I understand you speak a little Beothuk," said Burke. "That should impress old Howahkan."

"Yes, sir, the Point decided that we weren't likely to fight the Germans or the French anytime soon, so they let us study Spanish and some Indian languages."

Major Burke swirled his empty glass. "The Point brass must have more brains than when I was there."

Burke and Wagner rocked slowly. Wagner drank from his glass. They stared into the cold fireplace. Wagner looked up at Major Burke. "My Beothuk isn't very good."

"Doesn't need to be," said Burke. "Begin in Beothuk, they will be impressed, then they'll switch to English. Many of the leaders speak pretty good English. Different tribes used to communicate by sign language. Now most of the chiefs speak passable English."

Wagner hesitated, looked at his hands in his lap and

fidgeted. "Sir, may I speak frankly?"

Major Burke looked up. "Of course. You can always speak frankly. I expect you to."

"I appreciate your trust in giving me this assignment, but I'm new here. Wouldn't somebody who has more experience in dealing with the Beothuk be better prepared than I for the posting?"

"No. I'm giving you the charge precisely because you are new here. You'll have fewer preconceptions. And misconceptions. You should be more open-minded than other officers who have more frontier experience." Burke pointed a finger at Wagner. "This may be the most important assignment of your army career. You could have a hand in setting the tone of relations between the Indians and the United States for years to come.

"We're not dealing with a savage here, Lieutenant. Howahkan is a respected leader in the Beothuk nation, one of the top men. With his leadership in this new confederation, he's even more important in Indian affairs." Burke paused. "He has also been to Washington."

Michael was stunned. "Washington!"

"Yes. Two years ago. The President wanted to talk with Beothuk leaders, and the tribe chose four to represent them. Howahkan was one of the four. Did you see the silver medal around his neck?"

"I did, but I couldn't make it out."

"That's a peace medal. Presented to him by the Great White Father himself."

"That's impressive," Wagner said. "I lived less than a hundred miles from Washington and never got there. The President never invited me to visit."

Major Burke smiled. "Well, you never caused enough trouble to warrant a peace medal." Burke stood, glass in hand, and walked to stand before the fireplace. Wagner stood. Burke stopped and turned to face the lieutenant.

"By the way," Burke said, "when you deal with Howah-kan, who might be smarter than both of us, try to be a little more subtle than you were with the woman at the meeting."

Wagner looked puzzled. "Sir?"

"My god, man, everybody in the room knew you wanted to crawl all over her." Wagner winced. Burke smiled.

"Yes, sir."

"On that point." There was no humor in his voice. "This assignment is critical. We're trying to prevent an explosion, and you're going to be sitting on the powder keg. Think with your head, not your privates. Stay away from her." Burke did not smile.

"Yes, sir. I understand."

"Damn," he said. "What's happening here? The world is turned upside down." He shivered and bent over the stacked logs beside the fireplace. "Now help me get this fire built. I'm freezing."

# CHAPTER FOUR

## The People

Major Burke and Lieutenant Wagner stood on the parade in front of the commandant's house. Wagner held the reins of his horse. A short distance away, out of earshot, Sergeant Clark sat his horse at the head of ten mounted troopers in a column of twos. The restless horses shifted side to side and were brought back in line by the soldiers.

Behind the troopers, four packhorses stood idly, shifting their weight from side to side. Their packs bulged with provisions and camp gear. Two mounted troopers each held the lead of a packhorse, and another was tied behind each of these. Next in the column was a wagon with two mules in harness. The wagon was filled, the mounted contents covered by a canvas cloth. The reins of a saddled horse were tied to the rear of the wagon. Bringing up the rear were ten more troopers in pairs. Every soldier in the column watched Lieutenant Wagner and Major Burke.

"Send a sealed dispatch weekly," Burke said, "more often if you need to. Howahkan said he would arrange it. They shouldn't be able to break the code, but nothing surprises me anymore." Major Burke smiled, but there was no humor in it.

"Yes, sir." Lieutenant Wagner saluted, and Major Burke returned the salute. Wagner mounted, and Burke stepped back. The lieutenant nodded to Burke and walked his horse over to Sergeant Clark and the column.

The lieutenant and the sergeant moved out, and the column fell in behind. The teamster shook his lines and pulled the wagon up behind the pack animals. Major Burke watched them go.

Lieutenant Wagner looked about the post and wondered when and in what condition he would return.

The trail ran down the middle of a broad valley between ranges of high hills. The floor of the valley was covered with thick two-foot tall switchgrass that rippled in the light breeze like a gray-green sea. A clear shallow stream flowed over a sandy bottom alongside the trail. Originally a game path, the trail had been widened and beaten down by the army patrols that penetrated Indian country as well as the increasing numbers of Indians who visited Fort Andrew Jackson.

The parallel ranges that defined the valley converged, and the trail entered a canyon. Wagner worried that the wagon might not be able to negotiate the confined trail, but the scouts who had briefed him on the journey had said nothing of an obstacle.

When they entered the canyon, the stream narrowed and tumbled over a rocky bottom. The canyon closed in, and the wagon almost scraped against the walls. Conversation among the troopers declined as they looked up the canyon walls that seemed to lean toward them.

Sergeant Clark continued to talk and laugh. Wagner wondered whether the sergeant's chatter revealed an unrestrained confidence that nothing could threaten the group or nervousness that something could.

Above the walls, clouds thickened and darkened, and a light rain began to fall. Troopers hunched in their saddles and pulled their hat brims down to cover faces. Wagner pondered calling a halt to break out greatcoats. He looked up the canyon walls to the dark sky. He frowned.

"Sergeant!" Wagner said.

"I see it," Clark said. He looked up to the peak.

At the top, a tiny figure stood near the edge of the precipice. His back was to the valley as he waved white semaphore flags, easily visible against the dark sky.

The canyon walls rose almost vertically from the dry streambed. The narrow defile was only ten feet wide. Sergeant Clark, riding fifty yards ahead of the column, stopped on the trail and waved to Wagner. Clark dismounted, and his horse lowered his head at the side of the trail.

When the column came up to Clark, his mount was still drinking from the small pool beside the trail. A spring of fresh water bubbled from the ledge above the pool, roiling the surface of the standing water. Troopers dismounted to water their horses at the pool and fill their canteens from the spring.

The watering finished, the troop mounted and proceeded. Once through the pass, the canyon walls receded, and the valley opened gradually. The streambed carried a shallow flow of clear water alongside the trail.

The orange evening sun dropped below the tops of the dark pines across the valley. Lieutenant Wagner and Sergeant Clark turned their mounts off the trail toward a flat where they had decided to pitch camp.

The next day, the column rode in a broad valley of lush buffalo grass. The trail was more clearly defined now and bore evidence of regular passage. Wagner and Clark rode at the head of the column, followed by the escort and the pack animals and the wagon.

Michael raised a hand to signal a halt. About one hundred yards ahead, five Indians sat their horses in the middle of the trail, facing the column. Wagner looked at Sergeant Clark. Clark nodded. Wagner signaled forward, and the column moved ahead.

The soldiers came up to the Indians, and Wagner raised his arm for a halt. The column slowed and bunched up before stopping as the troopers paid more attention to the strange circumstance of greeting Indians peacefully in their own country than to military bearing.

Lieutenant Wagner and the Beothuk looked each other over. The lieutenant was at the same time curious and nervous. These were the first Indians he had seen other than those that hovered about military installations.

The Beothuk wore breechclouts, fringed leggings and buckskin shirts. Each warrior held a rifle cradled in the crook of his arm, a finger near the trigger. Wagner tried to appear casual when he glanced at the rifles. They were sleek and light, like no rifles he had ever seen.

The warrior in the middle, about thirty years old, was lean and muscular. He walked his horse forward a couple steps.

"Hello, friend," Wagner said to the warrior in heavily accented Beothuk.

The warrior responded in Beothuk: "You are welcome!" Wagner wondered whether the crisp response was typical of the Beothuk manner of speech or whether it was spoken in anger. This was the first time he had heard Beothuk spoken by a native speaker. His instructor at the Point, a soldier, had learned his Beothuk from native speakers during his trading days. By the time his Beothuk reached Wagner, it was heavily diluted.

The warrior turned to the Indian at his side. "All right," he said in Beothuk.

"Yes, Maloskah." The Indian rode to the wagon and stopped beside the driver's seat. The soldier stared at the Indian a moment, clearly unhappy with the whole affair. Looping the lines around the brake handle, he climbed down from the wagon. He scowled at the Beothuk, walked to the back of the wagon and untied the reins of his horse. He mounted and rode to the rear of the column.

The warrior rode to the back of the wagon and dismounted. He tied his horse's reins to the back and walked to the front. He climbed up to the driver's seat and untied the lines. He looked at Maloskah and nodded. Maloskah reined his mount around, squeezed his knees, and his horse moved off. The other warriors followed.

Lieutenant Wagner spoke to Sergeant Clark. "You are in command."

"Sir!" Clark responded. He saluted smartly, and Wagner returned the salute. The lieutenant turned his horse and followed Maloskah. The Indian in the wagon seat shook the lines and pulled the wagon into place behind Wagner.

After riding a few steps, the lieutenant turned to see the escort riding down the back trail, followed by the packhorses and their handlers. It was the first time he had felt alone.

The trail gradually widened. That it was heavily used was evident by the multitude of tracks and tracks on tracks. The trail converged with a wide, shallow stream whose banks were thickly bordered with willow and an occasional huge cottonwood. The trail left the stream and ran gradually up the slope of a low ridge. On a flat at the top, the party stopped.

Wagner was stunned. Below lay the principal village of The People. Tipis lay in hundreds along one side of the stream. My God, he thought, how many are there? Four hundred? Five hundred? How many more around the bend of the stream in the distance? He felt his head spinning.

Tipis were erected on a grassy bottom, all facing eastward. Fifteen to twenty tipis lay on each side of a lane that ran parallel to the stream. The stream and lines of tipis, some obscured by huge cottonwoods, extended hundreds of yards to the bend in the stream and beyond.

Scattered among the tipis, there were a few apparently permanent log and plank structures. The village had a more settled look than he had been led to expect. He wondered whether the Beothuk had given up moving with the seasons. Above the village, a forest of lodgepole pines, named for their use as support poles for tipis, provided home and cover for animals and a windbreak for the village.

The watercourse was marked by tall cottonwoods and thick stands of willows. On the other side of the stream, a large herd of hundreds of horses grazed on the lush bottom grasses. Near the stream, scores of horses were tethered, each by a leather line tied above a hoof and anchored to a stake.

Maloskah urged his horse forward, and the others followed. The loaded wagon brought up the rear. On entering the village, Wagner's astonishment grew. *This is not what I expected,* he thought. Tipis and the ground around them were clean and in good order. People stopped what they were doing and walked to the edge of the lane. They were quiet, watching the party pass.

Maloskah pointed to a long log building above the line of tipis. "Latrine," he said. Wagner smiled to himself at the English name. But why not, he thought? An adopted name for an adopted convenience.

The party rode by a large arbor covered with leafy vines. Just off the lane and near the stream, the arbor was constructed of small logs for the posts and willow shafts for the roof horizontals. Ivy covered the top and the western side that caught the hot afternoon sun. Benches and a table were made of hewn planks joined by wooden dowels.

The arbor was a gathering place. Women sat on the ground and on benches at tables of hewn planks. Some of the women wore cradleboards on their backs. The babies wrapped securely inside slept or contentedly looked at whatever appeared in their world, a view that changed as the mothers moved about. Other cradleboards and their plump burdens were propped against the columns that supported the arbor cover. The baby carriers were richly decorated in intricate patterns of colored quills and glass trade beads.

Small children played at the feet of the women. Three toddlers rolled on the ground with a fat little puppy, laughing wildly. Two small boys held their tiny bows as their fathers had instructed and tried to shoot their miniature arrows at a scampering puppy who was enjoying the game as much as they. The pup lowered his body on his front legs, then mock charged the boys, then rushed aside and ran away, only to turn and drop down on his front paws again, his mouth open in what appeared to be a broad smile, his tongue waggling.

The women watched the riders pass, whispering to each other. They paused in their quilling and beading to watch the spectacle of a wasichu soldier in his bizarre clothing riding at ease and undisturbed through their village.

The riders approached a large circular structure, partly underground. The portion above ground was built of stone and logs. The roof of hewn planks and thin logs inclined upward to a peak in the center. *It looks like a kiva,* Michael said to himself. *What the hell is a kiva doing in a Beothuk village?* He remembered the confederation, and the kiva made more sense. Howahkan and three other men stood beside the structure. Michael recognized the young woman who stood behind them. He resisted the temptation to smile.

The horsemen reined in beside the kiva and dismounted. One of the warriors took the lieutenant's and Maloskah's reins and led their mounts away. The wagon driver tied the lines around the brake handle and climbed down from the wagon. He walked to the back and untied the reins of his horse. He followed the warrior on foot with the other horses.

Maloskah walked over to the group at the kiva, nodded to Howahkan and stopped beside the woman. He spoke softly to her. She nodded.

Howahkan nodded to Lieutenant Wagner. "You are welcome," Howahkan said in Beothuk. "You are welcome," he added in English.

"Thank you, Howahkan," said Wagner in Beothuk, then switched to English. "Major Burke sends his greetings. And these gifts." He gestured toward the wagon. Howahkan nodded without looking at the wagon.

"We hope your coming to us will be good for your people and for our people," Howahkan said.

Wagner glanced often at the girl as Howahkan spoke. When Howahkan stopped speaking, Wagner quickly looked back at him. "We wish the same. There should be no conflict between us." As he spoke, he made glancing eye contact with the girl. She looked at him blankly.

Howahkan noticed Michael's interest in the girl. He frowned and turned to look at her. She looked down.

"This is Kimimela," Howahkan said. "She will show you our village. She will teach you our ways and answer your questions."

Kimimela stepped up beside Howahkan. She nodded to Wagner and stepped off toward the lane. The lieutenant looked at Howahkan, unsure what to do. Howahkan motioned for him to follow. Wagner hurried to catch up.

Howahkan watched them go. He turned to Maloskah and gestured toward the wagon. They walked to it, and Howahkan pulled back the canvas cover. They saw iron hatchets, iron pans and pots, skinning knives, blankets, cloth, glass beads and trinkets.

Howahkan shook his head. They spoke in Beothuk. "Maybe we should give gifts to the army." Maloskah smiled. "Give these to the people who have been hurt by the wasichus," Howahkan said. "If you need more, take from our stores."

"Our stores are low," Maloskah said.

"Yes. We must replenish. I fear the wasichus will soon try to move into our lands in many places. Unless we can impress the young ambassador with our strength."

Kimimela and Lieutenant Wagner walked down the lane among the scattered tipis. He glanced at her, but she looked down at the lane and ignored him. Women paused in their work to watch them. The women whispered to each other as the two passed. The men were less passive. Some of the men stared, curious about this white man, this wasichu soldier, though they had been told of his coming.

Others glared and frowned, hostility on their faces.

Olaktay, a warrior, passed them, walking in the opposite direction. He frowned at this strange spectacle of a uniformed wasichu in his village, then stopped and glared at Wagner's back as he walked by.

Wagner tried to speak Beothuk to Kimimela. He labored, straining for the correct words. "I am happy . . . here. Thank you . . . me . . . here." *God, how ridiculous I must sound.* He had never attempted communicating with a non-English speaker before, and he was struggling more than he had expected. *Is it the language or Kimimela?*

Kimimela looked at him. She did not smile. She replied in Beothuk. "You are welcome. We hope for a good result. But I doubt that you will do anything useful here." She looked down at the roadway.

Wagner frowned. He shook his head, confused. He had understood nothing. He looked around at the village. Okay, he would try again.

"You . . . live here . . . long time?" he said haltingly in Beothuk.

Kimimela stopped walking, and he stopped. She sighed and looked up at him. "Not bad for a soldier, I suppose, but perhaps we had better speak English." She had spoken in English with hardly a hint of an accent.

Wagner's jaw dropped, and his eyes opened wide. "Wha— you speak English!"

"Yes. This is yours."

They stood before a new tipi. Tanned buffalo hides were stitched neatly together and stretched over a conical framework of slender lodgepole pine saplings about twenty feet long. The poles converged at the peak where an opening provided an escape for the smoke from an interior fire. The tipi was anchored to the ground with pegs driven through slits at the bottom of the hide cover. The door of buffalo calfskin was partially closed with short willow sticks, tapered at one end, that were inserted through holes. The bottom half of the door was open.

Wagner bent and stepped through the opening. Kimimela followed. Inside, Wagner straightened and looked around. The ground was covered with clean buffalo robes and a black bear skin with claws still attached. A rawhide line for hanging clothing was tied between two tipi poles. Two empty parfleches hung from pegs that had been tamped into holes in poles. The stiff rawhide carrying bags, about two feet by three feet, were painted with colorful geometric designs. Two backrests made of willow sticks and tanned skins were pushed against a tipi wall.

Wagner was surprised to see an army-style wood-framed bed against a wall. He smiled when he noted, happily, that the standard mattress stuffed with moldy hay was absent, replaced by thick buffalo robes with the hair left on. His bag of clothing and personal items rested on the floor at the foot of the bed. A small wooden desk and chair were pushed against the wall near the head of the bed.

*Where did they get this stuff}* "Where did—"

"If you need anything, tell me," Kimimela said. She turned to go, pushed the tent flap aside, stooped and went out. Wagner hurried after her.

Outside, Kimimela stepped into the lane, intent on getting away.

"Kimimela," called Wagner.

She strode away. "Tell me if you need anything," she said, without looking back.

"Kimimela! Where can I find you?" Nothing. She did not respond or look back.

# CHAPTER FIVE

## Kimimela

Wagner and Kimimela strolled on the village lane. He stole glances at her as they walked. She wore a dress made from supple elk skins, lightly embellished with quill embroidery. A leather belt tied around her small waist bore simple geometric designs. Her knee-length leggings and moccasins were decorated with colored quills and beads. Wagner's colorful uniform was plain and drab in comparison.

They passed two women who stood at a cooking fire. One tended strips of venison impaled on green skewers that slanted over the flames. The other woman stirred stew in an iron pot that lay in the embers. The women nodded to Kimimela. They stared with unabashed curiosity at Wagner. He smiled at them.

Kimimela and Wagner walked on. They stopped and watched five women sitting in a circle on a blanket beside a tipi, laughing and chattering. One of the women rattled dice in a wooden bowl.

"They try for a winning combination of seven," Kimimela said. "Before, we used plum stones with markings."

Kimimela stepped off, and Wagner hurried after her. After just a few steps, Kimimela held up a hand, signaling a stop. She looked across the stream where the horse herd grazed on the lush bottom grasses.

"Look over there," she said. Between the herd and the stream, six young bareback riders pulled the reins of their horses, circling and milling, round and round, back and forth, jockeying for position.

"Watch," Kimimela said. The horses lined out and burst into a furious gallop on the flat along the stream bank. "They like to race," Kimimela said. "Watch the girl on the big gray." The horses ran in a bunch, appearing to be a perfect match. Then the girl on the gray pulled ahead.

"She always wins," said Kimimela. "It makes the boys angry."

Wagner smiled. "I can understand that. No man likes to be bettered by a woman." He smiled.

Kimimela glared at him. She was not amused. He smiled.

Wagner and Kimimela stood in a clearing in the lodgepole forest above the village. It was quiet here, except for the muffled sounds that rose occasionally from the village below. Each held a bow, and each wore a quiver of arrows. Wagner examined his borrowed bow. It was strung and ready for use.

Kimimela readied her bow. The sinew string of the bow was fastened with a loop at the notched end. She pulled the loose string until it had reached the desired tension and tied the string at the other end of the bow. She pulled the string to test it for tautness. Wagner watched this process with surprise, then curiosity, and finally admiration.

She looked up and noticed his attention. "What?" she said.

He smiled. "Nothing," he said. "Now what?"

Kimimela pointed across the clearing at a tree about thirty yards away. A small stretched skin was tied to the trunk at eye level. She faced the target, holding the bow with her left hand. She reached over her shoulder, found an arrow and pulled it from the quiver. She notched it on her bowstring, pulled with no apparent effort, aimed at the skin and released. The entire process took place in what seemed a blink of an eye.

The arrow struck the skin. She turned to Wagner, her face expressionless.

Wagner reached over his shoulder, felt around for an arrow, felt again, looked back over his shoulder and found one. He pulled the arrow from the quiver and notched it.

"You look . . . strange," Kimimela said. Wagner frowned. This whole affair is strange, he thought to himself. A uniformed United States Army officer playing at archery with a Beothuk girl in a Beothuk village. He shook his head.

"Do you need help?" she said.

He looked at her and smiled. He still held the notched arrow. He raised the bow, pulled the arrow to the feathers, aimed at the skin, and released. The arrow struck within an inch of Kimimela's arrow.

She jerked around and glared at him. She pulled another arrow from her quiver, notched it, aimed, pulled and released. The arrow struck a couple of inches from her first arrow. She turned toward him, her chin raised slightly.

Wagner pulled an arrow from his quiver, notched it, pulled the bowstring, aimed and released. The arrow struck a couple of inches from Kimimela's second arrow.

Kimimela looked at him, scowling. "Where did you learn this!" It was more an accusation than a question.

"At the Point," he said. "It was a popular recreation."

"The bow is a weapon, not a toy."

He smiled. "Yes, but—"

Three shots rang out in rapid succession from behind and to the left side. The skin target was ripped to shreds.

Kimimela and Wagner whirled around to look toward the shots. As they turned, Michael reached for the pistol at his hip and drew it. Kimimela brought up her bow and reached over her shoulder for an arrow. She had hardly grasped the arrow when she released it.

They saw Olaktay lowering his rifle. Olaktay laughed. Then he glared coolly at the lieutenant and Kimimela, turned and sauntered away.

• • • •

Howahkan, Maloskah, Kimimela and two others stood at the hitching post beside the kiva. "Food projections are satisfactory," Howahkan said. "Goods are low. And armaments. We must go to Gold Mountain." The others nodded.

"Grandfather," Kimimela said, "what do I tell the wasichu soldier of our absence?"

"He must not know of Gold Mountain," said Maloskah.

Howahkan pondered a long moment, staring blankly across the valley. The others waited in silence.

"If we continue on the road we have traveled for many winters," Howahkan said, "we will continue to fight the army and the wasichu settlers. We may win, but we may not. Many will die." He turned to face the others. "Now we have an opportunity. We must gamble. Ambassador will go with us to Gold Mountain."

The others were shocked and made to protest. Howahkan held up his hand for silence.

"It is done," Howahkan said.

Howahkan and thirty other warriors stood beside their mounts. They checked harness and fittings and slid rifles into cases. Four warriors checked the stiff, buffalo-hide panniers of eight packhorses. The baskets were lightly packed, less than half full.

Kimimela and Wagner stood nearby. He wore his army uniform. Kimimela tied a bandanna around his head, covering his eyes. "If this slips," she said, "you must tell me. If anyone suspects that you can see, there will be trouble for you."

The lieutenant leaned toward her and spoke softly. "Kimimela, if I could see you, why would I look at the trail?" She tightened the bandanna with a jerk.

"Ouch," he said.

She took his arm and led him to his mount. He bumped roughly into the horse. She placed the reins in his hand, and he swung up into the saddle.

"I will have the lead rope on your horse," she said. "You must keep a loose rein." She mounted, and the two horses bumped together. Wagner leaned toward Kimimela.

"I have had dreams of being in the dark with you," he said, "but not exactly like this." She frowned, squeezed her mount with her knees, and moved off. The lead rope on Wagner's horse tightened, and they rode toward the others.

Howahkan turned his mount onto the trail, followed by the warrior escort. Kimimela pulled into line, with Michael in tow. The four warriors leading the eight packhorses fell in behind them.

Howahkan's party rode on a lightly traveled trail in a meadow of tall buffalo grass. Michael was enthralled with the wild smells and bird song. He tilted his head backward, trying to see under the blindfold.

"No!" Kimimela said. He recoiled at her voice. She had by chance turned to look at him the moment he tried to see under the blindfold. "You must not do that! Some of the men had wanted to put a . . . what do you say ... a hood over your head. That would not be comfortable. If they see you trying to look, they will do it. Please."

She reached over and pulled the bandanna lower, lightly brushing his cheek with her hand.

"I'm sorry," he said. "I'll be good." In fact, he was mesmerized. It was the first time she had touched him.

After a few miles, the trail inclined gently upward into the foothills. When they entered scattered stands of bur oaks and bigtooth maples, they split into a number of files to find their separate paths. Through breaks in the foliage, the riders saw the high mountains that loomed ahead. Tree line was visible where the green of conifers and deciduous trees gave way to bare gray hillsides of stone and scree.

Kimimela glanced at Wagner. He rode with head lowered. The bandanna was still firmly in place. Her face betrayed no emotion.

The party rode in single file on a rough trail above tree line. Snow lay in shaded patches alongside the trail. The only sounds were the squeak and clink of saddle fittings and the horses' hooves on the stony trail.

Kimimela turned to look at Michael behind her. He rode with his head down and hanging like a pendulum, moving side to side with the gait of his mount.

When the trail widened, she reined her horse off the trail and pulled his horse up beside her.

"Are you okay?" she said.

"Okay," he said, his head still hanging. He raised his head and looked toward her though he could not see her.

"Kimimela . . . would you touch my hand?" He extended his hand toward her.

"What?" she said.

"Just touch my hand. Please."

She frowned. But she reached out and lightly touched his hand. He pulled his hand back and faced forward.

A rough camp was pitched in the lee of an almost vertical wall of rock above the tree line. Dirty snow lay in patches around the narrow flat. The wall of stone across the canyon was painted an ethereal orange tint by the dying sun. It gave an illusion of warmth that did not dispel the increasing cold as the temperature dropped. Deep shadows etched a tableau of black and gray in the campground.

Members of Howahkan's party milled around, making camp.

A few warriors worked on two fire pits. Others opened mule packs and pulled out dry sticks that they had gathered in the forest below. Horses were tied to a rope strung between rock outcroppings.

Lieutenant Wagner sat on the ground near a third fire pit, leaning against his saddle. The bandanna still covered his eyes.

A warrior bent over the pit. He blew on moss and splinters, making smoke, then tiny flames as the dry wood caught fire. He arranged small sticks around the flames and some larger sticks on these. He looked up at Kimimela who stood behind Wagner. She nodded. He stood and walked away. Kimimela bent down and removed the bandanna. Wagner sat up and rubbed his eyes.

"What a relief!" he said. He looked up and saw the brilliant orange rock face across the canyon. He turned back to the front and exhaled deeply. He looked around the camp, then turned to see Kimimela behind him. "What is this place?"

"A place to camp," she said and walked away.

The embers of the campfire glowed bright red and yellow in the darkness. The firelight cast dancing shadows on the stone walls. Warriors lay on the ground near their fires, covered by skins and blankets. Wagner lay near the fire, covered by a colorful wool blanket. He looked across the fire at Kimimela. Only the top of her head was visible above the blanket.

She stirred, then pulled the blanket below her eyes. She looked directly at Wagner. They made eye contact a long moment. She blinked sleepily, then curled up until she disappeared into her covers.

Wagner lay back and stared into the black void.

The barren high country was behind them, and they rode on a faint trail through an aspen grove. The canyon had opened, and slopes strewn with huge boulders slanted upward from the flat.

Boulders also were scattered about the flat, the result of hillside erosion or an ancient cataclysm.

The horses walked with heads down, nibbling at the short, dry grasses, the first grass seen since entering the high country. The riders kept their mounts moving with some difficulty. Wagner and Kimimela rode side by side behind the escort and before the pack animals. Wagner's shrouded head bobbed with the rhythm of his mount's gait.

Shots rang out ahead from both sides of the trail. The warrior riding beside Howahkan lurched backward and fell from his saddle. The other riders slid quickly from their mounts, pulling rifles from cases, and took cover behind boulders.

Kimimela reached for Wagner. She grabbed his shirt-sleeve and pulled him roughly from his mount as she slid to the ground, holding his arm to break his fall. She whipped the bandanna from his head and pulled him to cover behind a large boulder. Wagner shook his head, trying to focus and clear the cobwebs. He leaned against Kimimela.

"Are you okay?" he said. She nodded. He looked up the hillside, searching for the shooters. Scattered shots from above struck boulders and ricocheted, whining overhead.

A voice shouted in Beothuk from the hillside, "Traitor! Howahkan! Coward! Traitor!"

Members of Howahkan's party aimed their rifles toward the voice and fired. More shots rang out from the slopes on both sides of the trail.

Wagner shouted to anyone in hearing range, "Give me a gun! I can shoot!"

Howahkan was crouched behind a boulder nearby. He shouted, "Kimimela!" She looked toward Howahkan. He heaved a rifle to her, and she caught it. Howahkan then tossed a small skin bag of bullets.

She handed the rifle and bag to Wagner. "It shoots six times without reloading," she said. His eyes opened wide.

Another shout from the aspen grove above: "Kimimela, are you there?" Kimimela jerked her head up and looked over the boulder toward the voice. She turned back to Wagner, her face hard.

"Kill him," she said.

Wagner looked toward the direction of the shout. He shouldered the rifle, pointed in that direction and waited. He saw movement from behind a boulder. He sighted and fired. The figure fell.

The same voice again from the grove: "Traitors! You betray The People!" Wagner and others fired toward the voice. Return fire from the groves and rocks above spattered the boulders on both sides of the trail.

The shooting declined and ended. Wagner and Kimimela and the others searched the walls for movement. An unseen canyon wren sang its cascading trill, then all was still.

Howahkan stood and looked upward. He held his rifle at the ready. Then he lowered the weapon and relaxed. Everyone stood, rifles held loosely, and looked around. Howahkan spoke to two warriors who went to the man who had been killed. They lifted him to the back of a horse and tied him there.

Satisfied that the body was secure, Howahkan took the reins of his horse from a warrior and mounted. The others mounted, the pack animals were assembled, and the party moved off.

# CHAPTER SIX

## Gold Mountain

The campfires cast huge shadows on the rock wall behind the camp. Members of the escort sat around two fires. Some cleaned rifles. Others prepared their beds. Three warriors picked up rifles and walked into the darkness to relieve lookouts.

Howahkan and Kimimela sat on skins in the circle of light at a third fire. Wagner sat on the opposite side of the fire, leaning against a downed tree trunk. They stared into the flames.

"We fight two enemies," Howahkan said, "the wasichus and our own people. Taloka calls me a traitor for seeking accommodation with the Americans. Taloka calls his band the . . . Patriots," he said in Beothuk. He looked at Kimimela.

"Patriots," she said in English.

"They say they want to live as they have always lived," Howahkan said. "They will not accept that the world has changed. The old ways were good, but the world has changed. We seek an accommodation that will protect the interests of The People in this new world."

"I understand," Wagner said. He stared into the flames. He glanced at Kimimela. Her face was hard.

Howahkan stood. He nodded to Kimimela and Wagner and walked into the darkness. Wagner watched the flames dance and listened to the crackling of the fire. He spoke to Kimimela without looking at her.

"How do you know Taloka?"

She did not answer immediately. She stared into the flames.

He turned toward her.

"He was a member of our band," she said, still studying the dancing flames. "We were childhood friends, played together. He was popular. His name, Taloka, means a friend to everyone.

"When the wasichus came, he changed. He had a vision, he claims he had a vision, that he will lead The People back to the old ways."

Wagner turned to stare into the flames. "How do you know him? Now."

Kimimela looked at the lieutenant. She turned back to look into the fire. She pondered, as if deciding whether to respond. "He thought I was betrothed to him. He tried to force me ... I refused. We fought. I cut him with a knife. Howahkan made him leave. Taloka said he would kill me unless I went with him."

Kimimela stood and walked away. The darkness swallowed her. Wagner watched the flames a moment longer, then stood and walked into the darkness in the opposite direction.

After relieving himself, he walked back to the fire. He stopped. His blankets were laid out next to Kimimela's. She lay in her blankets, the cover pulled up to her chin. She looked up at him.

He sat down on his blankets and removed his boots. He lay down and pulled a blanket up to cover him. He rolled over to face Kimimela. They looked into each other's eyes. A sweet moment.

Wagner leaned over to her. He kissed her on her mouth, softly, tentatively. She did not resist. They kissed lightly again.

"What am I to call you?" she said softly. "I will not call you 'Lieutenant Wagner.' Soldiers' names are bitter on my tongue. I won't call you 'wasichu' anymore." She smiled thinly. "I will call you 'Ambassador.' "

He winced. "I wish you would call me 'Michael.' "

She smiled, frowned, snuggled into her blanket and closed her eyes.

• • • •

Howahkan's party rode in a narrow valley, about a hundred yards wide. The walls on each side of the valley rose almost vertically to craggy peaks. The trail, shaded by aspens and pines, lay alongside a fast-flowing shallow stream.

Howahkan raised his hand to signal a halt. He nodded to the rider at his side. The warrior pulled a short-barreled, large-bore pistol from his belt. He pointed it skyward and fired.

A small projectile shot high into the air. The flare exploded and shone brightly as it arced to a peak, burned out and disintegrated.

The riders moved off, single-file.

The shallow stream became a rushing torrent, tumbling over boulders that jutted from the streambed. The riders made their way slowly down the rocky trail on the gentle slope. The trail descended to a level and widened, showing evidence of the passage of many horses.

Ahead, two Beothuk sat their horses in the middle of the trail. Howahkan's party came up to the men, and Howahkan signaled a halt.

"Hello, friends," Howahkan said.

"You are welcome, Howahkan, you are expected," the guard said.

"All is well?" said Howahkan.

"Yes, Howahkan."

Kimimela pulled the lead rope of Wagner's horse until he was beside her. She reached over and removed the bandanna from his head. He blinked and rubbed his eyes.

The two scouts turned their horses and moved down the trail. Howahkan and the others fell in behind them. They followed the trail alongside the stream, which now was about thirty feet wide. The lazy flow disappeared into a broad, deep pool. At the bottom of the pool, the stream flowed over the edge and tumbled down a cascade of boulders. At the base of the falls, the stream widened and slowed. They rode on, the canyon walls receded, and the valley opened to a wide meadow. The shallow stream continued to spread, and the flow slowed again.

Wagner looked around in disbelief. "Kimimela, this is amazing!"

Ahead of them, on the left side of the stream, a flat meadow of knee-high grass stretched five miles away to a range of low hills. A herd of about fifty sleek horses grazed in the lush green grass on the flat alongside the stream.

Across the stream, the grassy bottom sloped up gently to a bench about a half-mile away where a number of substantial frame structures stood. Thin smoke plumes rose from chimneys atop some of the buildings.

Wagner was surprised to see men standing in the

streambed. Howahkan reined in where ten men stood in the shallow water, about eighteen inches deep, holding round, shallow pans. The water was crystal clear, revealing the shimmering bottom of smooth pebbles. The men were dressed in loose cotton shirts and pants that looked like canvas pajamas. They wore round conical hats made from what appeared to be dry reeds.

Wagner was dumbstruck. He had not seen many Asians anywhere, none since crossing the Mississippi.

Howahkan spoke to the men. "Wei, peng you men. Jin tian zhao dao da de jing kuai mei?" Hello, my friends. Are you finding large nuggets today?

The men smiled broadly. "Yi xie xiao de jing kuai huo hen duo jing pian." Some small nuggets and many flakes, said one.

Howahkan smiled, pulled his mount back from the bank and proceeded on the trail. The others fell in behind.

Wagner leaned over to Kimimela. "What did they say?"

"I don't know," she said. "I don't understand Chinese." He frowned. She smiled, enjoying his confusion.

Howahkan turned his mount into the shallow water at a ford. The party splashed across the stream and pulled up on the other bank where three men stood, waiting. They smiled broadly.

Howahkan and the party dismounted. Howahkan shook hands with the three men. The men nodded in deference to him. Wagner studied the men. They were dark-skinned, like the Indians, but they were dressed in white men's clothes.

The men turned to Kimimela. One of the men smiled broadly to her. "Es bueno verte otra vez, Kimimela," he said. "Tú sabes que te amo con todo mi corazón y quiero huir contigo a mi páis." It is good to see you again, Kimimela. You know I love you with all my heart and want to run away with you to my country. The man's companions guffawed. Kimimela smiled.

"Estoy lista irme contigo, Jesus," Kimimela said. "Pero qué hacemos con Maria?" I am ready to go with you, Jesus, but what do we do with Maria?

The man feigned disappointment. "Ah, se me olvidó de mi esposa. Pues, probablemente no puedes hacer tortillas como Maria." I forgot about my wife. Ah well, you probably cannot make tortillas like Maria's.

Kimimela feigned disappointment in return. "Lástima pero no puedo. Ahora, Jefe, miramos a la mina?" Alas, no, I cannot. Now, Jefe, shall we look at the mine?

The Mexicans and Kimimela smiled. Wagner frowned. The others in Howahkan's party listened to this exchange, puzzled, understanding nothing.

The Mexican turned to go. "Vengan conmigo, por favor." Come with me, please. He gestured for the others to follow. Wagner remained, unsure what to do. Kimimela stopped and turned toward him. She saw his expectant look.

"Come on," she said. "You might as well see it all."

# CHAPTER SEVEN

## Come Back, Kimimela

Jefe, Howahkan, Kimimela and Wagner stood near the mouth of a mine tunnel, looking into the dark passage. Two pairs of iron rails emerged from the tunnel mouth on a smooth, crushed-rock roadway. The rails curved to the right on a flat bench, rounded an outcropping and were lost to view.

As they watched, an Indian materialized from the darkness. He held the lead of a mule that pulled an iron cart on the rails. As the cart passed, Wagner saw that it was loaded with large rocks. Ore, he guessed. On the other pair of rails, an Indian led a mule that pulled an empty cart toward the tunnel mouth.

Kimimela and Jefe spoke in Spanish, and she translated for Howahkan. The noise of the mine works drowned out their conversation. The three wandered away from Wagner as he watched the ore carts.

Wagner started to walk over to them, but Kimimela held up a hand to discourage him. He stopped. He watched Kimimela. He had never known anyone who was so sure of who she was, so capable and in control. Who was in charge here? He caught her eye. She looked at him blankly and revealed nothing. Did he know her at all?

Wagner turned to his right. He listened. A muffled, rhythmic pounding sound came from that direction. He frowned.

"Que? Uh, what?" Kimimela said. She had walked over and stood behind him. Wagner started in surprise and turned to her. He saw Howahkan and Jefe walk into the tunnel mouth and disappear into the darkness.

"What is that noise?" he said.

Kimimela walked toward the pounding sound. She beckoned for him to follow. He caught up, and they walked beside the iron rails toward the noise. They passed a loaded ore cart pulled by a plodding mule that rolled in the same direction. On the other parallel tracks, an Indian led a mule pulling an empty cart toward the mine tunnel. A stream beside the roadway tumbled down a rocky gorge.

The pounding sounds grew louder and louder until it seemed the mountain itself would crumble and fall on them. They rounded an outcropping where the rails curved around a bend.

Wagner stopped in his tracks. His eyes widened. "What th—"

Kimimela laughed. "Have you never seen stamp mills?"

They stood before a row of ten heavy vertical iron rods that were fitted loosely in a frame so that the rods could slide up and down. A mechanism raised each rod in turn and released it at its maximum lift. The heavy iron shoe fitted at the bottom of each rod fell heavily on the ore and water mixture that had been placed on a base under the rods.

"Stamp mills," said Wagner. "I've heard of them. I understand there were stamp mills at gold mines in North Carolina, but I never saw one."

"The Mexicans brought these from Mexico in pieces," Kimimela said.

"From Mexico! How . . . did Mexican officials know about this?"

"Of course not!" she said. "The officials would try to prevent anybody, including The People, from challenging their hold on the country. They had just seen the Russians leave."

Wagner looked blankly at her.

Kimimela wrinkled her forehead. "You don't know about the Russians."

"Well, I know that they tried to expand their settlements from Alaska, but, no, I don't know much about Russians in California."

"They settled on the northern California coast. They tried to farm and trap furs. But they were not successful, and they sold the property a few years ago and left. The Mexican government was glad to see them leave."

Wagner shook his head and smiled.

"What?" she said.

"You amaze me."

She looked puzzled. "Why?"

"Never mind," Wagner said. "Transporting the stamp mills here must have been very difficult."

"Yes. But they had help. From an American. He is a big merchant in Monterey. He's also your government's representative to California."

"A consul?" Wagner said.

"Yes, I think that's what they called him. He demanded a lot of money, and we paid him. He arranged the transport on one of the ships that carried his goods from Acapulco. They landed the parts on the northern California coast."

"The north coast," Wagner said. "Away from Mexican

customs officials. They smuggled the mills into California. The consul would know how to do that."

"Well, yes. Our people met the ship and helped the Mexicans bring the parts over the mountains on mules."

Wagner shook his head, wondering at the enormity of the task.

They watched the mill stamps lift and drop, lift and drop, crushing the chunks of ore at the base.

"How are they powered?" he said.

"Water. From the stream here. The flow is not always reliable, but we have the ability . . ." She looked out at the valley.

"What?"

She hesitated. "I don't know how much I can tell you."

"I don't understand," he said.

She inhaled deeply. "You are Ambassador. But you are also a soldier and a wasichu."

He looked into her eyes. "I would never do anything to hurt you."

"Even if ordered by your commander?"

Wagner hesitated. He reached slowly toward her cheek. She turned aside quickly and looked around furtively.

"No. We must go." She stepped back on the roadway and walked toward the mine tunnel. Wagner watched her a moment, then followed.

A full moon described soft outlines of a row of small cabins constructed of logs and hewn planks. Wagner and Kimimela stood a short distance downhill, between the stream and the low end of the line of cabins.

"We leave early tomorrow," she said.

"Where will you sleep?" he said.

She motioned toward the cabin at the upper end of a

row. "I am in the women's cabin," she said.

He reached for her and pulled her to him. He held her face with both hands. They kissed lightly.

"Stay with me," he said. "I am alone in the men's cabin."

"I cannot . . . Michael." She leaned into him and kissed his lips softly. She turned and walked slowly up the hill. Before she had gone far, she stopped and turned back to look at him. The moonlight outlined the soft contours of her face, a face that betrayed no emotion.

Michael looked up at her. "Come back," he whispered to himself.

She turned and walked with hurried steps up the hill.

• • • •

The morning sun cast beams of golden slivers through the branches of the trees on the nearby slopes. The only sounds were a sweet mixture of bird song and the gurgling of the shallow stream over the pebbly bottom.

Michael and Kimimela sat on the grassy bank. She stared at the stream.

"Look!" she said. She pointed at the disturbance in the water where a trout had broken the surface of the stream, lunging for an insect. She looked at him. He was staring into her eyes.

"Michael, you didn't look," she said. She turned away.

He smiled and took her hand. She frowned, withdrew her hand slowly, smiled and looked at her feet.

He studied her face, her hair, her eyes. "I dreamed of you," he said.

"You had a bad dream?" A smile played about her lips.

"Yes. I chased you, and you ran from me."

"What happened?"

"You disappeared," he said.

She looked at her hands in her lap. She looked up at him. "Then what happened?"

"I woke up. I got up and went outside. I walked up to the women's cabin. I stood there. I sang to you to bring you out to me. I willed the good spirits to disturb your sleep and bring you out." He smiled.

She looked down at her hands. "Don't talk like that."

They looked at the stream where trout swam lazily below the bank. They watched two colts in the meadow across the stream cavorting like playful children. A fresh breeze brought the sounds of the mine to them. Michael looked up the hill.

"Tell me about the mine," he said.

She turned to him, grateful for a change in the conversation. "The People have operated the mine for about ten years now."

"What do you do with the gold? Where do you spend it? I haven't seen any gold at the post store."

"We spend it for the benefit of The People," she said.

Michael frowned, pondered. *Is it time?*

"Kimimela, I must ask. Where do The People get the repeating rifles? And the flares and the exploding weapons?"

She looked up at him. Her face revealed nothing. She looked across the stream at the meadow. "Don't ask me that. You know I cannot tell you."

He leaned toward her. "If I am to help avoid trouble between The People and the Americans," he said, "you must trust me."

"You have been in our village only a month. Have we not shown that we trust you? Howahkan has told you about his hopes for an understanding with the Americans so we can live in peace side-by-side. Now he has shown you the gold mine. I can tell you nothing about the weapons.

Grandfather will tell you what he wishes you to know."

"Grandfather?"

"Howahkan is a respected leader. And my grandfather."

He pondered a moment. That explains a lot, he thought to himself. "I understand that he has been to Washington. Did you go with him?"

"No," she said. "He said I could come if I wished. Not because he needed me, but for the experience. I didn't want to go. I would miss my people and my village too much. I did not wish to go away again."

"Again? What—"

"He didn't like Washington. He said that the people he talked with knew nothing of the world beyond the fences of their city. They pretended that they knew about The People, but they knew nothing. He said they never listened and never asked questions. They only talked and talked.

"He also said that everything smelled bad. The streets, the food, the air, the people even. He said he longed for the sweet smell of the columbine and wet buffalo grass."

"So he learned nothing useful and regretted the trip?" he said.

"Oh no, he said he learned much. He saw big buildings, wide hard roads, wagons loaded with all kinds of things, things to eat and wear and machines and tools. And people. So many, many people. He wondered how The People could resist the Americans. He said that he had seen the beginning of the end of our way. He was very sad."

Kimimela looked up the hill. She stood up. "They are coming," she said.

Michael followed her glance. Howahkan and Jefe walked toward them. The members of Howahkan's escort followed. Behind the escort, four Indians led the eight pack mules. Their panniers were bulging. And heavy, judging from the way the packs swayed.

Michael stood and watched the procession coming down the hill. He grimaced. Unanswered and unasked questions rocketed around in his head.

Howahkan's party rode single-file on the narrow trail above tree line. The rocky canyon walls loomed on each side of the trail.

Kimimela held the lead rope on Michael's horse. She turned to look at him. The bandanna blindfold was wrapped securely around his head. His head bobbed up and down, side to side, as his mount negotiated the rocky trail.

As Howahkan's party approached the village, people ran out to welcome them. Howahkan nodded to them and raised his arm in greeting. Others emerged from tipis when they heard the greetings, and they added their welcomes. After exchanging greetings, the riders moved off in different directions toward their tipis. The warriors who led the packhorses continued riding toward the kiva.

Howahkan, Kimimela and Michael dismounted at the hitching rail beside the kiva. Nalokshni, an elder of the village, approached Howahkan. "Howahkan, these men wish to speak with you." He gestured toward three Americans dressed in homespun who stood near the kiva entrance. They looked expectantly, a bit nervously, at Howahkan.

Howahkan walked over to them and extended his hand. The men relaxed, smiled and shook his hand. The four walked to the kiva and went inside.

Michael had watched Howahkan and the visitors with interest. When they disappeared inside the kiva, he turned to Kimimela, puzzled. "What are they doing here?" he said. "Are they Americans?"

"Mormons." She fussed with her horse, loosening the girth. She untied a pouch from her saddle. "They settled last year in the Valley of Salt Water. They want to join the confederation."

He frowned. "Mormons. A troublesome lot."

She looked up, frowning. "Troublesome? Are all who resist the wasichus troublesome?"

"Yes. You in particular. You trouble me. You trouble my sleep."

She stroked her horse's neck, a hint of a smile on her lips.

"On that point, can we find another . . . term?" he said. "Wasichu is pretty harsh."

She giggled. "Oh, you no like wasichu. You white man! You wasichu!"

"Okay, squaw woman!" He looked around. Who was looking? What he really wanted to do was grab her and kiss her and hold her. But all he could do was stare at her and want her. She understood his frustration, smiled and backed away.

They strolled toward the kiva entrance. They stopped when they saw the three Mormons walk from the kiva. The Mormons walked toward their horses, which were tied to the rail behind Michael and Kimimela. The Mormons stopped in front of Michael. They looked him up and down.

"Are you army?" said one, who appeared to be their spokesman. He had been first to approach Howahkan. "What are you doing here?"

"I was invited," Michael said. The Mormons glared at Michael. "And you?" Michael said.

"Not by invitation, but we are welcomed."

"Are you welcomed by the tribes who live in the Valley of Salt Water?" Michael said.

"We live at peace with the Ute people."

"You don't have a reputation for peace," said Michael. The Mormons stiffened. Kimimela glared at Michael.

"With God's help," the Mormon said, "we defend ourselves from those who persecute us."

"Why do you want to join the confederation?" Michael said.

"The enemy of our enemy is our friend," the Mormon said.

Kimimela looked fiercely at Michael, then turned toward the Mormons. "You are welcome," Kimimela said. "You come in peace. I hope our leaders admit you to the confederation." The Mormons stared wide-eyed at this Beothuk woman who spoke flawless English.

The lead Mormon recovered. "Thank you," he said.

The Mormons scowled at Michael a long moment, then turned and walked to the hitching rail where their horses were tied. They untied their reins, mounted and walked their horses down the lane.

When the Mormons were out of earshot, Kimimela turned to Michael and spoke sternly to him. "You make trouble."

Michael smiled.

# CHAPTER EIGHT

### Going to Grandmother's Land

The flap of Michael's tipi was thrown back, and sunlight streamed through the opening. Inside, the tipi was in good order. The bed was made up, army style. The top blanket was stretched taut, side-to-side and top-to-bottom. His few possessions were neatly stowed in the bag at the foot of his bed and under the bed.

He sat in the chair at his desk. He held a paper bearing a plain-language message addressed to Major Burke. He read:

"I think I have won the trust of Howahkan. Still have no clear understanding of what he expects of me. Have seen source of their wealth, gold mines that they control. Have no knowledge of the source of armaments. Michael Wagner, LT, U.S. Army."

He reached into the desk and took out a code card and a blank sheet of paper. He took a pen, consulted the code card and began to write the coded message on the blank paper.

Michael stood with Maloskah near the kiva entrance. He wore his uniform, a bit rumpled and creased from lack of attention and cleaning. He handed a pouch to Maloskah and spoke to him. Maloskah nodded and entered the kiva. Michael turned and faced the morning sun. He looked up at the sky and inhaled deeply, savoring the crisp, clear new day.

He strolled down the lane. Women who worked around their tipis smiled at him, or nodded to him, or scowled at him, or ignored him. Two women looked up from their cooking fire and leaned toward each other, talking softly, and giggled. He smiled at them.

When he reached Kimimela's tipi, he stopped, pondered going to her. As if on signal, she emerged from the opening, bending. When she had passed through the opening, she stood upright and saw him. She smiled.

"Good morning, Michael," she said in Beothuk. He said nothing. He simply looked at her. He took a step back the way he had come and waited. She stepped up beside him, and they walked down the lane.

"Did you sleep well? No bad dreams?" she said.

"No bad dreams."

"Are you comfortable?"

"I have never been more comfortable or more at peace," he said.

She smiled. He moved closer to her. She moved away and almost imperceptibly shook her head. She looked furtively around. He smiled. He knew that the Beothuk do not show affection where others can see, but he liked to tease her. She could not always tell when he was teasing.

"I'm still not sure what Howahkan expects of me. Can you tell me?"

"I don't question him. He will talk to you when he

wishes."

She looked at his feet. He wore moccasins.

Howahkan, Maloskah and two others stood outside the kiva. They listened to a warrior who talked excitedly to them. He held the reins of a horse that was lathered and blowing.

Howahkan spoke to Maloskah who ran down the lane toward Michael's tipi. The others disappeared inside the kiva entrance.

The dying sun beyond the wooded hills cast long shadows across the valley. A mounted force of two hundred warriors rode in good order through the knee-high grass. They were armed and painted for war. Howahkan and Maloskah, followed by Kimimela and Michael, rode at the head of the force. Michael wore all Indian clothing.

The campfires on the broad prairie were like fireflies in the darkness. Blankets and skins and bags were scattered about in the circles of light. Warriors sat around fires, cleaning rifles and sorting cartridges as they recounted stories of past battles. They chewed pemmican, the convenient food favored by hunters and travelers, made of dried buffalo meat, dried berries and fat.

Howahkan, Maloskah, Kimimela and Michael huddled around a small fire. Howahkan leaned toward Michael who sat across the fire. "The people we go to help are being forced from their land," Howahkan said. "They have lived there and hunted there for thousands of winters. Now the Americans say they want the land, and they tell the people they must go to another country and live in a small place that they do not know. The people refuse, but they are losing the fight. Why do the Americans do this? Do they believe they own all the earth?"

Michael stared into the fire. He looked up at Howahkan. "I . . ." But he could say no more. How could he answer this question for Howahkan when he was finding it increasingly difficult to answer it for himself?

As long as he could remember, he had believed like virtually every other American that his country was destined to expand to the Pacific Ocean. It was only a matter of time. The native inhabitants were part of the wild land that would be conquered in time. They had no legitimate right to the land. They would either be beaten down or reach an accommodation with the Americans. That this was inevitable he had never doubted.

But now? His musing was interrupted by Howahkan's voice.

"When the American explorers came to our country in my father's time, your Captain Lewis said that the Americans wanted peace and wished to trade with us. But when it suits the Americans, they decide to forget promises. When Americans come to plow our land and soldiers come with their guns, this is not the way to peace."

There was a long silence as they stared into the dancing flames.

"What will these people do now?" Michael said.

Howahkan leaned back. He looked hard at Michael. "They know they cannot hold their land, this land of their ancestors. So now they try to go to Grandmother's Land where the Americans cannot harm them."

Michael frowned. "Grandmother's Land?"

Howahkan looked at Kimimela. "Canada," she said.

Howahkan turned to Michael. "You go with us to watch. Watch and remember."

Howahkan's force rode at a lope through a broad prairie toward a range of low hills in the distance.

Ahead, a band of about one hundred mounted painted warriors sat their horses quietly beside the trail. They waited as Howahkan's force rode by them. Then they urged their mounts forward and fell in behind.

Howahkan led the band of warriors, now numbering three hundred, on a trail that snaked through a narrow, deep canyon. The evening sun had disappeared behind the canyon walls, and the trail lay in heavy shadow. At a point ahead where the trail widened, a hundred painted warriors sat their horses. When Howahkan's force had passed, the warriors fell in at the rear.

The sun was high as the combined body of four hundred warriors rode at a lope in a broad valley between ranges of low hills. Howahkan and Maloskah rode at the head, occasionally leaning toward the other to speak. Michael and Kimimela rode behind them. Michael leaned forward in his saddle to catch the conversation, but he could make out nothing. He could only hear hoof beats and excited mutterings from the riders behind him.

The warriors were restless. Their excitement grew as they anticipated the coming battle. They talked loudly, shouted, chanted. They brandished their weapons over their heads. Most carried rifles; some held spears or war clubs.

Howahkan held up his arm to signal a halt and pulled up. Sporadic rifle fire sounded in the distance. There was still no visible evidence of the battle, no combatants or smoke.

Howahkan spoke softly to Maloskah. Maloskah wheeled

his horse sharply and galloped down the column. He was back in a moment. The two leaders of the other warrior groups rode up behind him. Howahkan spoke to the three.

One of them wheeled his horse and shouted a command down the column. He kicked his horse ahead into a gallop on the right, angling away from the column. Immediately his hundred warriors raced after him.

The other leader wheeled to the left and shouted down the column. He burst into a gallop, angling off to the left, and his hundred charged after him.

Maloskah signaled the remaining two hundred warriors forward. The column moved out in good order at a lope.

• • • •

A furious battle was in progress. A long line of soldiers lay and kneeled behind the crest of a low rising. They fired down on Indians who were huddled behind the low embankments of a dry streambed. The besieged warriors fired at the army line from their poor cover. Under the embankment, children cried and clung to their mothers.

Casualties lay exposed in the creek bed. The wounded moaned and cried for help. Dead horses lay in the dry bed. Wounded horses screamed as they rolled and struggled to rise. Belongings were strewn about the sandy creek bottom. Blankets, pots, parfleches, tipi poles, hides, clothing, every piece a family possession.

Howahkan's force of two hundred arrived on the outskirts of the battle. They hurriedly dismounted, tied their reins to scrub, and crept up to the skirmish lines. They took cover behind large rocks and hummocks and fired at the army's lines. Some soldiers shifted their positions and fired on the newcomers.

Following the first volley from the army lines, there was

a brief lull as the soldiers reloaded. Warriors in the front rank of the Indian lines also stopped firing. Heads raised, they listened. They heard a rumbling of hooves, first softly, then growing in intensity. Warriors looked toward a low ridge where the sounds seemed to be concentrated.

A cavalry unit of eighty soldiers galloped around the point of the ridge. They charged straight toward Howahkan's force, sabers raised.

The cavalry had hardly cleared the ridge when a force of a hundred warriors burst into view from the right and charged the cavalry force at a gallop. The warriors fired repeating rifles as they came. Sabers in hand, the soldiers could not return fire.

The two mounted forces collided and fought hand to hand from horseback and on the ground. After a furious five minutes of brutal combat, soldiers and warriors broke apart and fell back from the skirmish. Each side tried to rescue their wounded as they fled the skirmish, and each side left their dead on the bloody ground. The survivors rode hard for their own lines.

Firing continued sporadically from the army and confederation lines. A cannon boomed from the army position. The shell exploded in the streambed, and bodies and materials flew into the air. Another burst from the cannon and another explosion in the streambed.

Two warriors from Howahkan's force crawled across the flat, hidden by scrub, toward the army line. Each dragged a tubular weapon. The two warriors rose slowly to their knees, still crouching, and raised the tubes to their shoulders. They pointed their weapons at the cannon, aimed and fired together. The two projectiles exploded on target as one. Cannon and cannoneers were launched into the air.

Warriors and soldiers heard hoof beats on the army's far flank and stared in that direction. The force of one hundred warriors who had ridden leftward from Howahkan's column swept over a rise and galloped toward the army line. They fired their repeating rifles as they charged.

Warriors in Howahkan's main force rose in the flat where they had hidden in brush and behind rocks. They threw barrages of grenades until the entire army line appeared to be erupting in smoke and debris.

The army was overwhelmed. Soldiers lowered their rifles. A white rag attached to a rifle barrel rose from behind the embankment. Down the line, another rifle with a white flag tied on lifted from the line. Firing from both sides ended. Soldiers, subdued and confused, stood with their arms raised. Warriors walked toward the army line, rifles at the ready.

Michael stood and looked at the army lines. He watched warriors walk among the soldiers who still held their arms in the air. Some warriors taunted the soldiers and shouted their victory, brandishing their rifles and spears.

Howahkan and Maloskah also walked among the warriors and the soldiers, calming the warriors and speaking to officers and soldiers. Soldiers lowered their arms and went to tend the wounded and collect their dead comrades.

Michael tried to assess his feelings. This was a spectacle he had never expected to witness. He felt the humiliation of the soldiers and their officers, surrendering to hostiles following an action that the army had initiated. He knew this was not an end, but a beginning. The memory of the event would stain the reputation of the unit and the army until it was avenged in blood.

He turned and looked at the embankment, which had been the fleeing Indians' protection. A woman held a baby, its face and blanket sprinkled with its own blood, rocking back and forth and wailing. Other women and men walked about the dry streambed, bending to pick up pieces of clothing, pots, baskets, weapons, anything that might be salvaged for the journey that must be resumed.

Kimimela stood beside Michael. She had watched him as he struggled to understand what had happened and what was happening to him. When he turned away from the field, she put her arms around his waist and held him close.

Michael and Kimimela sat on the stream bank below the village arbor. The evening was quiet, still. Only an occasional sound was heard, a muffled shout from the village, a pony whinnying in the field across the stream.

They watched the gentle flow of the stream, the ripples over the shallows. A dozen ducks, disturbed by something in the cattails, burst as one from the stream and flew away, dripping and complaining.

"What will happen now?" Kimimela said.

"The army won't forget," he said. "It's all about honor and pride."

"It wasn't the soldiers at your fort."

"It's the same army," he said.

"We could have killed them all. But we let them go. Their commander said that they would not interfere with The People again."

Michael avoided her glance. "He had no authority to say that. It means nothing. He was trying to save his men's lives. Howahkan surely knows this. I hope Howahkan's victory, and his mercy, is not lost on the army and Washington."

They watched the languid flow of the stream. Small eddies formed where the bank jutted out into the flow.

The water was clear as crystal, and the pebbles on the bottom were only slightly obscured by the ripples that disturbed the surface.

"Leaders all over the plains and mountains talk about what the future holds for them," Kimimela said. "Some will fight change, but others who know what has happened to tribes east of here are afraid.

"Last summer, grandfather went to a council of confederation head men. They talked about the question of change and how to deal with it. Some said that the confederation would be strong enough to prevent change. Others were not so sure, even with their advantages.

"Grandfather said that one Cheyenne chief said that he was going to ask the Great White Father to send him one thousand young white women as brides for his young men. He said that since the children of these marriages would be Cheyenne and white, soon the Cheyenne and whites would be one people."

She looked at him for a response. He continued to stare at the stream. "Well, what do you think?" she said.

He turned to her. "Beothuk men love to gamble, don't they?" he said.

She looked puzzled. "Yes. They will bet on anything."

"Here's a sure thing. Don't bet on the Cheyenne." She smiled. "Okay, I will tell them." She threw a small stone into the stream. Circles spread from the splash, outward, outward, rippling outward. "Maybe peace will spread," she said, "like that." She pointed at the circles, still moving outward from the pebble splash.

# CHAPTER NINE

## You Are Exasperating

The buffalo plains. A scattered herd of about two hundred buffalo grazed undisturbed in the flat plain, lush with tall buffalo grass that waved rhythmically in the light breeze like a slow ocean swell.

Michael and Kimimela sat their mounts on a flat rising above the plain. Four warriors and one woman sat their horses nearby, watching Michael and Kimimela. They spoke softly among themselves. The woman leaned toward a companion, giggled and covered her mouth with her hand.

Michael wore moccasins, an Indian shirt and army trousers. He was astride Kimimela's horse. The horse had been trained for the buffalo hunt. She was riding her grandfather's buffalo horse.

Most Beothuk men and some women had horses that were trained and ridden for specific purposes. In addition to the horses that comprised his wealth, the typical warrior owned a buffalo horse, a warhorse, and a horse for general riding and moving camp. The fortunate warrior might also own a prize racing gelding. This mount was so highly valued that he might be picketed at the owner's tipi door.

Kimimela's horse, Michael's mount, wore an Indian saddle. Michael had been a little apprehensive when he saw the saddle and wondered whether he should switch it for his own army saddle, but he did not wish to appear ungrateful. So he relented and left the saddle on. He was surprised when he found the saddle quite comfortable. He said so to Kimimela, and she had explained how it was constructed.

It was made of two pieces of wood about twenty inches long and one and a half inches thick. The two pieces were held together by two Y-shaped pieces of elk horn, one piece at the front and the other at the back.

This wood and horn frame was covered with green buffalo hide that was sewn together with sinew. When dried, the whole was rigid and comfortable for rider and horse. The girth and stirrup straps were also of buffalo hide. Stirrups were of rawhide and wood.

"Did you make it?" he said. *Why not? She is a marvel. She does everything. Why shouldn't she make saddles?*

She laughed. "No. Certain men make the saddles. Grandfather had this saddle made for me when I was eighteen. I didn't know whether it would be good for you, but it looks okay. You have nice hips, I mean narrow hips."

She looked down, embarrassed. He smiled. "I'm glad you like it," she said.

Kimimela's horse was not saddled. She and the men were skilled hunters and rode bareback. The other woman rode a saddle similar to Michael's.

Each person held a bow and wore a quiver of arrows on their left side at the waist. All but Michael's arrows carried markings that identified the hunter. This identification was not so important in a hunt such as this, with only a few hunters. They were most useful in a large hunt when a great number of hunters would need to be able to claim their kills at the end of the hunt.

"Are you sure you want to do this?" Kimimela said. "You could watch."

"I've watched twice," he said. "I want to do it."

"You could use your rifle."

"No."

She frowned. "You are ... I don't even know the word!"

"Exasperating?" he said.

"Yes! I think so. You are exasperating!" she said, scowling.

She pulled her reins hard, causing her horse to shy sideways. She recovered control and walked her horse away. Michael squeezed his knees and walked his horse up beside her. The other riders fell in behind.

She glanced at him, frowned, and looked at the buffalo. Two animals on the edge of the bunch had stopped grazing. They stood stiff-legged, looking at the riders.

"You're going to get yourself killed," she said, without looking at him.

"One less wasichu." He smiled.

She glared at him. "You!" She kicked her horse into a furious gallop. Michael raced after her. The others followed at a gallop. Kimimela reined sharply to the right and dropped over the edge of the rising. The others followed, flowing down the slope. At the bottom, the hunters lined out and galloped across the plain toward the buffalo.

The buffalo were aroused by the approach of the riders and began moving away, slowly at first, then at a lumbering lope. Before the hunters reached them, the buffalo were in full gallop.

The hunters strung out, running in a line parallel with the stampeding buffalo. Each rider held a bow. The rider in the lead edged his galloping mount close to a running bull. His horse almost touched the buffalo. Holding his bow with his left hand, he put his reins between his teeth, reached to his left side and pulled an arrow from the quiver. He notched it, aimed a couple of inches above the front leg joint and released. The arrow struck home, plunging into the flesh up to the feathers. The buffalo collapsed and tumbled. The rider veered left to avoid the rolling animal.

A young rider who had swerved wide to avoid the rolling carcass gradually moved his mount back to the galloping herd. He edged close to a large cow. He was about three feet from the animal when he pulled an arrow from his quiver, notched it, aimed and released. The arrow plunged into the belly, behind the leg joint, not a killing shot.

The buffalo swerved sharply toward the rider. The cow bellowed, lowered her head and charged the horse. She struck the horse in its midsection, narrowly missing the rider's leg, and jerked her head upward, goring the horse in its belly. The horse was thrown sideways, and horse and rider tumbled. The buffalo swerved back to the rampaging herd, the arrow flapping in its side.

Kimimela kicked her horse hard in the flanks and drew up beside the wounded buffalo. She pulled an arrow from her quiver, notched it and pulled it right up to the feathers. She aimed it at a point just above the buffalo's front leg joint and loosed the arrow.

The arrow struck home and disappeared, going all the way through the body. The buffalo collapsed and rolled. Kimimela's horse shied to avoid the tumbling buffalo. She slowed her horse and turned back to see the young rider standing beside his downed horse.

Michael and the others raced ahead alongside the stampede. Michael drew up beside a galloping bull. He put his reins in his teeth and reached across his body to his left side for an arrow. He didn't find it, felt again, found an arrow and grasped it, and lost it. He reached again, found the arrow and pulled it from the quiver. At that moment, the buffalo lowered its head and swerved leftward toward Michael's horse, forcing him away from the herd. Michael struggled to hold reins, bow and arrow without losing any.

The buffalo veered back toward the herd. Michael took the reins from his teeth and followed, kicking his horse hard in the flanks. He edged closer to the bull, his mount now almost touching the buffalo's side. He returned the reins to his teeth, notched the arrow he held and pulled the shaft.

His mount was bumped hard from behind, and he was almost jolted from his saddle. He shouted and turned just in time to see the war club swinging toward his head. He lurched sideways, and the rider who had pulled up alongside him landed a hard blow on his shoulder. Michael dropped his bow and arrow and almost lost his seat.

The two horsemen raced ahead, slanting away from the stampeding animals. The assailant swung again and landed a glancing blow to his head. Michael shook his head and felt as if he were spinning. He recovered and swerved his horse toward the attacker, bumping his mount and almost unseating him. The attacker closed on Michael and swung again, striking a glancing blow to the head. Michael gripped his horse's mane as his head whirled.

Michael shook his head again, and his vision cleared. He saw his attacker raise the club, then drop it. He was being lashed about the head and shoulders. The warrior raised his hands over his head to protect himself.

It was Kimimela. She had galloped up beside him and

struck him repeatedly in the face and about the shoulders with her quirt, then the face again. His face was marked and bloody from the lashing. The attacker turned his galloping horse from Michael toward Kimimela. He grabbed the quirt, pulled it from her, and threw it away. He drew a knife from his waist.

Michael swerved his horse toward the attacker. He drew a pistol from his hip holster and aimed at the assailant. The attacker saw the pistol and whipped his horse sharply sideways and galloped away. Michael raced after him.

Kimimela shouted, "No, Michael! No! Come back! Taloka!"

Michael whipped his horse after Taloka. He gradually gained on him. He aimed his pistol and fired. Missed!

Taloka galloped toward a low rocky outcropping at the edge of the plain with Michael still gaining on him. Five Indians on foot stepped slowly from behind the outcropping. Taloka rode straight for them.

Michael saw the five and reined in hard. His horse slid to a stop. He watched as Taloka reached the five. They stood their ground, staring at Michael.

Michael whirled his horse and galloped back toward Kimimela.

# CHAPTER TEN

## You Are Early This Year, Little Friend

Michael and Kimimela strolled among the horses tethered on the grassy bank near the stream. They stopped beside Michael's army mount. The horse nickered and threw his head up and down in recognition. Michael stroked his back.

Every warrior owned a number of horses that were his joy and comprised his wealth. All of the horses were part of the large herd that grazed on the lush meadows that bordered the stream.

But every warrior kept a particular horse near in case he should need a mount quickly. These were the horses that were tethered closest to the stream and near the ford. Michael's horse was tethered here for the same reason.

Kimimela rubbed the muzzle of Michael's horse. "You are not safe here," she said. "Taloka has spies in the village. He will know everything you do. Everything we do. His strength grows with each person who leaves us to go to him. Many people, many in the village, believe as he does. The people want peace, but not a peace that requires us to become wasichus, Americans."

Michael reached for her hand and held it. She looked up at him and slowly withdrew her hand. They looked across the stream at the village where people walked in the lane, sat under the arbor, stood at cooking fires and went about daily tasks.

A shadow seemed to have fallen across Kimimela's face. "There is much talk. Many people think Howah-kan no longer represents The People. Some still think we should fight the wasichus wherever we find them in our country."

A small, neat log cabin lay in a prairie as flat as a griddle. About thirty yards from the cabin, a line of scrub willows and a dense thicket of wild plum trees suggested a water-course, though no stream could be seen from the house. Between the house and the stream, a small field of yellow wheat glistened in the bright sunshine.

On the other side of the house, a man, seemingly in his forties, though he might have been ten years younger, chopped weeds in a large vegetable garden. He paused, straightened and flexed his back. He pulled a bandanna from his pocket and wiped the sweat from his face. He admired the fruits of his labor and pondered its promise. There were tomato plants, beans, potatoes, squash, beets and carrots.

An orchard of two dozen two-year-old fruit trees flour-ished in the flat beside the line of willows. A few trees still bore the spent remnants of blossoms: pears, cherries, apri-cots and plums. A single wild chokecherry shrub nearby wore clusters of fragrant white flowers. He had removed a number of small chokecherry trees during his spring clearings since the leaves at his last farm had sickened his horses and cattle. When this one began to flower, he hadn't the heart. He would watch his stock and cut it later.

The woman, about the same age as her husband, hung out clothes on a line stretched between a willow pole and a peg notched in the cabin wall.

Busy with their work, they heard the riders before they saw them. Five mounted Indians painted for war galloped through the shallow stream, spraying the grassy verge and themselves.

The man dropped his hoe and the woman the shirt she held, and both ran frantically toward the cabin. A charging warrior felled the man with a rifle shot before he left the garden. Another rider killed the woman with his hatchet before she reached the cabin doorstep.

The Indians dismounted. While one held the reins of the others, two went to the wheat and the other two to the house. They quickly made fire, and the field and the cabin were soon blazing. They watched until they were sure the fires had caught well. Then they mounted and galloped away.

The dugout home was built into the slope of a low hillside. A log construction extended the dwelling about five feet from the face of the hill. The roof peak was just about high enough for an average-size man to stand upright without bruising his forehead.

A gray-haired woman in a plain bonnet and soiled apron stood a few paces away from the doorway of the dugout. She watched a thin old man in sagging overalls who struggled with a plow behind a gaunt mule. The blade cut into the grassy sod and turned it over, revealing rich dark soil. He was enlarging a garden that already showed promise in the young plants.

The farmer pulled the mule to a stop. He sighted down

the furrow and wrenched the plow blade a bit leftward. Then he looked up and saw the Indians. The four warriors, their faces and upper bodies painted, walked their horses across the meadow toward the dugout.

The old man raised his arms and face to the heavens and began to pray. "Oh Lord, save us like you saved Daniel from—"

Before he could finish his plea, the Indians were walking their horses over the tender plants of his garden. The old man saw the club that the lead warrior held at his side and crossed his arms over his head. The warrior swung the club and broke the old man's arm and crushed his skull.

Another warrior charged toward the woman. He rode her down and killed her with a club. She fell backward through the dugout door.

The Indians fired the logs of the dugout extension. They looked around and saw nothing else to burn. They rode their horses through the garden again and galloped away, yelling.

The two neat log cabins lay side by side. Near the cabins, a large, flourishing vegetable garden was surrounded by the beginnings of a living fence. In the spaces where the fence plants had not yet taken hold, brush was piled and intertwined to keep out animals.

Beyond the garden, a stout corral of stripped poles enclosed three sleek horses. On one side of the corral, a log lean-to provided shelter for the animals against bad weather. Past the corral, there was a field of wheat and an orchard of fruit trees that bore the dry petals of spent blossoms and a few new green leaves.

In the garden, a young farmer plowed behind two stout mules. Another man worked on a partially raised barn near the corral. Two women stood in the yard between the cabins where clotheslines were strung. Three toddlers played on the ground nearby.

The six painted Indians made no pretense of stealth, rather terror. They galloped into the compound, shooting their rifles as they came.

The women scooped up their children and fled for the cabins. The farmers ran for their rifles, lying on the ground where they worked. None reached safety. The men were shot down before they could reach their weapons. The warriors killed the women and children with clubs and hatchets.

The Indians dismounted and took scalps. They made fire quickly with their flint and torched all of the buildings, even dismantling the corral. They set the wheat field afire with some difficulty. The wheat was still green, but dry from lack of rain.

The brittle stalks smoked, caught fire, popping and crackling. The Indians fanned the flames with robes, and the field blazed. They watched the structures and the field burn, shouting their victory. Then they mounted and galloped away, yelling and waving the scalps.

A cluster of a dozen agitated Beothuk warriors stood outside the kiva. Maloskah spoke rapidly to Howahkan.

Michael strode toward them. Howahkan watched him come and waited in silence. He was grim.

"Ambassador, some of your people have been attacked. There have been deaths. It was Taloka. I have sent men to the villages of The People everywhere to tell them what he has done. You must write to your Major at once. Tell him that The People did not do this thing. I will send your letter at sunrise."

Michael glanced furtively at Kimimela. He turned back to Howahkan.

"I will bring it to you at first light." He turned and strode away.

About fifteen tipis lay randomly on the grassy banks of a shallow stream. Three buffalo hides were stretched and staked beside tipis. Women kneeled on the hides, scraping the skins with chisel-shaped fleshing tools. Other women tended cooking fires and stirred pots of stew. Racks beside tipis held strips of meat for drying.

Behind the village, three old men groomed horses, chatting and laughing. Beyond the old men, about thirty horses were loosely picketed on the grassy stream bank. Between the old men and the horse herd, two boys rode their horses around and around until one fell to the ground. The boy still mounted and the men laughed as the unhorsed boy clambered up and laughed with them.

Some young boys splashed in the shallows of the stream near the tipis. Three little girls sat on the bank playing with dolls. The dolls were made of buckskin and stuffed with hair. One girl wore a miniature baby carrier on her back. The fuzzy head of a doll poked out from the top of the carrier.

The only sounds were the soft splash of water, the murmurings of the children and the laughter from the direction of the horse herd. And a mountain bluebird that called in the distance. A woman at a fire straightened and looked in the direction of the mellow whistle. *You are early this year, my little friend. What does this mean for us?*

As if in reply, the peaceful tableau was shattered by the rumbling sounds of hooves. The women and children looked up to see a wall of mounted soldiers with sabers held high, galloping toward them.

The old men who had been with the horses ran toward the village, but before they reached it, the troopers were galloping among the tipis where they slashed at the terrified women and children and fired their pistols on them. The men from the horse herd arrived only to be cut down with the rest. All were killed in the melee. Men, women and children.

Soon all was quiet again. Tendrils of smoke from the cooking fires swirled in the light breeze.

The bluebird called again in the distance.

The soldiers walked their horses through the lifeless village, wending their way among the bodies. Leaving the village, the troopers passed a small American flag that fluttered from its willow staff tied to a pole of a burning tipi.

Michael emerged, bending, from his tipi. He straightened and rubbed his eyes. He smelled and heard the crackling of new fires, sensations that he had come to anticipate each day.

Then he straightened. Kimimela stood in the lane before his tipi. He had not noticed her when he came out. She had a blank look. Or was it sadness?

"Kimimela, what are you doing here so early? Are you okay?"

"It is too late," she said.

"Howahkan said sunrise."

"Soldiers attacked a village," she said. "They killed everybody. Children."

"My God!" he said. "Taloka! Did they get him?"

"Of course not!" she said. "He would not expose himself. He wants this! The village was peaceful. It was convenient. They were close to the fort, less than a day's ride. Michael, they flew the American flag. They had been told to fly the flag, and they would not be harmed."

"I'm sorry, Kimimela," he said. "I can't explain. Some Americans do not wish to deal with Indians. Maybe the officer thought they were hostiles."

"Children!"

"There were children at the farms," he said softly.

"Your farmers were killed by savages," she said, "not by The People! Don't you understand!" She choked back a sob, whirled around and stormed away.

The floor of the tipi was covered with skins and blankets. Michael sat on a blanket holding a small writing desk. A candle lantern on the ground near him cast a bubble of light in the darkness, softly illuminating the ground coverings and the tipi walls. The upper walls and peak were dark.

This posting was Michael's first opportunity to use the lap desk. His father had used it during his service as government surveyor along the trans-Appalachian frontier. When Michael graduated from West Point, his father had passed it to him.

"You'll have desk work to do," his father had told him, "but you'll not likely do it with a roof over your head."

His father had been right. At sixteen inches wide, ten inches deep and four inches high, the desk was the right size for slipping into the pannier of a packhorse or stored with other gear in a wagon.

Michael rubbed the polished surface lightly, remembering. He opened the narrow hinged panel at the top to reveal pens and an inkwell. There was also a single lead pencil, which Michael viewed as a curiosity and never used. He selected a steel nib pen.

He lifted the larger hinged writing panel and took out a blank sheet. He lowered the panel, dipped the point into the inkwell and wrote in plain English on the paper:

"You and your peers must distinguish between those who seek peace and those who do not. On both sides of the frontier. Your enemy on this side of frontier is renegade Taloka, not The People. You will know who enemies of peace are on your side of frontier."

He lifted the hinged desktop again and took out a code card and a blank sheet. He closed the top and laid the blank sheet between the code card and his handwritten message. He tilted the desk slightly toward the candle lantern to illuminate the papers.

He consulted the code sheet and began to write the message in code.

The morning sun cast long shadows of trees and tipis before the kiva. Michael and Maloskah stood at the hitching rail outside the kiva entrance. Michael handed a small pouch to Maloskah.

"I will send it now," Maloskah said.

"Thank you. Is . . . Kimimela here?"

"She goes to see her kin," Maloskah said. "Do you understand?"

Michael frowned. He nodded and turned to go, head hanging.

"Ambassador!"

Michael stopped. He turned back to see Howahkan striding toward him.

"Come with me, both of you." Howahkan said. He

turned and walked away. Maloskah and Michael followed.

Howahkan, Maloskah and Michael rode their horses at a slow lope through a prairie of knee-high grass and wildflowers. Six warriors rode after them. Rifle stocks projected above their cases. The horsemen rode around a low ridge and stopped abruptly. About fifty yards away, the remains of the tipi village still smoldered. Howahkan walked his horse, and the others followed.

They stopped at the edge of the village a moment. Then they walked their horses slowly in the wreckage, wending their way among the burned tipis, scattered possessions and carcasses of horses.

They rode to a small copse of willows on the stream bank. A number of upright scaffolds leaned against the slender willow trunks. Each scaffold, comprised of four poles lashed together into a frame, held a body. A few of the scaffolds held objects that had been important to the deceased. But those who had erected the scaffolds had found few intact personal possessions in the wasted village to comfort the dead in the spirit world.

The horsemen sat their horses quietly. They looked long at the scaffolds. Then Howahkan turned his horse and walked him through the village. The others followed.

At the last tipi, Howahkan stopped. The small American flag hung limply on its thin staff. Howahkan leaned over and removed the flag from the willow. He pushed the flag into a skin bag at his waist and kicked his horse into a gallop. The others galloped after him.

Howahkan's party rode at a walk through a thin wood of scattered scrub oaks. The wood ended, and the trail stretched ahead down the slope into a broad prairie. The riders kicked their horses into a lope.

A few scorched timbers were all that remained of the dug-out dwelling and the dreams of the old couple. The bloated carcass of the mule, still attached to the plow, lay in the ruined garden. Dry fragments of plants were strewn about.

Howahkan, Maloskah, Michael and the warriors sat their horses quietly before the two graves, side by side. A gust of wind raised a soft rustling in the tall prairie grass behind them and set the dust of the new graves swirling. Simple board crosses were pushed into the ground at one end. One of the crosses leaned to the side.

Michael got down from his horse and walked to the graves. He bent down and straightened the leaning cross. He pushed it down a few inches into the soft soil to steady it upright. He stood there a moment, then mounted in a hurry and moved off at a lope. The others followed.

Michael sat on a blanket in the center of his tipi. Sunlight from the open flap illuminated the writing desk that lay on his crossed legs. He held a pen and bent over the desk.

A coded message and code card lay on the top of the desk. Below the coded message, the decoding in plain English was almost finished. He consulted the code sheet and wrote the last line of the message.

He set the desk aside and picked up the decoded message. He read:

"Give me intelligence, not lectures. Am pressed by superiors, now by Washington. Patience grows short. You say this side of frontier and your side of frontier. Remember your place and your charge. What is the source of armaments?"

Michael crumpled the message tightly. He stopped, pondered, then slowly smoothed the paper on the top of the desk. He opened the desktop and put the message and code card inside. He closed the top, lowered his hands slowly to his lap and stared at the tipi wall.

The moonlight from the open flap softly illuminated the interior of Michael's tipi. He slept on the ground under his blankets.

He stirred at a brushing sound at the flap opening. The moonlight was obliterated a moment by a shadowy figure. Michael sat up quietly and picked up the pistol that lay on the ground at his side. He watched as the figure, now inside the tipi, turned back and pulled the flap down, but the flap remained ajar. A sliver of moonlight lay across Michael's blankets.

Michael aimed the pistol at the figure. "Who is it?"

"Don't speak," Kimimela whispered. She kneeled beside him. She kissed him lightly on his mouth.

Michael laid the pistol on the ground beside him. He pulled her to him and held her tightly. He whispered in her ear. "I thought I had lost you."

She put her hand lightly over his mouth. "Shh. Don't speak," she said. She stood and removed her dress, dropping it to the ground. She loosed the ties of the leggings where they were tied below her knees and stepped out of them. She kneeled, lay down beside him and slid under his blanket.

# CHAPTER ELEVEN

## We Might Be Cousins

The stream where it flowed by the village was about twenty feet wide. It was deep here, as much as five feet in places. A few hundred yards below the village, there was a ford where it widened and was only a foot deep. It was here, on the upstream side of the ford, where the women washed clothes. It was a dependable stream, never running dry. Even in years when there was little rain, the springs in the distant mountains that fed the stream continued to issue from the rocky hillsides.

Kimimela sat on the grassy bank above the stream. Michael stood behind her. They watched a trio of plump little cliff swallows swoop erratically and dip down to the water to skim insects from the surface. The late evening sun behind the village cast long shadows over the bank and stream and into the meadow beyond.

"Did you enjoy your visit with your kin?" he said.

She pulled her knees up and laid her chin on them. "I wasn't visiting. I was running."

"Running? From what?"

She turned and looked up at him. She sighed, exasperated. "From you," she said. "Do you understand nothing?"

Michael smiled. He sat down beside her.

"Kimi, stay with me in my tipi. Can you do that?"

"No. No one must know."

He reached over and took her hand. "I don't know whether I can manage that," he said.

She slowly withdrew her hand. "You must, or I must go away."

He leaned back on the grassy bank, raised up on an elbow. He looked at her back. "You could still go to Mexico with Jesus," he said.

Kimimela whirled around and looked sharply at him. "Michael!"

"We had a housekeeper when I was young who spoke no English. She was given to my parents by an acquaintance, a Cuba trader."

"Given to you! You owned a slave!" she said.

"A few. Most Virginians of any position own slaves," he said.

"That's disgusting," she said. "To own a human being like an animal."

"Oh? Some tribes take captives from other tribes and force them to live with them. The Beothuk do this, I believe."

She narrowed her eyes and glared at him. "That's different. Most are adopted by someone in the tribe. Especially when a child is taken to replace a child a woman lost. They are not slaves."

"Are they free to leave?"

She stared hard at him. She dropped her gaze and looked at her lap. "The People do not do this now. Except those who hold to the old ways." She softened. "How many slaves did you have?"

He lay down and put his hands behind his head. "Around fifteen or so usually."

She watched the ripples in the stream where a fish had surfaced. "Did you have any women . . . young women?"

He smiled behind her back. He knew where this was going. He had fielded the question many times at the Point and at army postings.

"A few," he said.

"Did you ever . . . did you ever . . ." She paused and turned to face him.

He smiled. "Bed a slave?"

"Did you?"

He pushed up on his elbow and sat upright. "No. But it isn't unusual. Some owners are just plain vicious, but some care for their slaves, not only as property, but also as human beings. Children, too. Owners' children and children of slaves often play together. They know nothing of servitude and color."

"Did you have slave playmates?" she said.

"I did." He looked away and stared across the stream toward the horizon. She noticed.

"It ended. It always ends," he said.

She waited.

"I had a playmate, a girl. My first childhood memories are filled with . . . Mary Anne. Her name was Mary Anne. Her mother was a house servant, so we were together most of the day. When I learned something, I taught her. She could read as well as I."

"Was she pretty?"

Michael hesitated. He looked at the stream. He pointed at a kingfisher that had alighted on a snag at the water's edge. It held a small fish in its beak. She looked, then turned back to him.

"Was she pretty?"

"Yes. She was."

"How old were you?" Kimimela said, "when it ended."

"We were the same age. Fifteen. It's one thing for small children to play together. It's quite a different thing for a slave owner's nearly grown child to be a companion of a slave child. Then my father saw us kiss. It was the first time, and he saw us."

"What happened?" she said.

"He wasn't unkind. He was apologetic. You see, Mary Anne was not just a slave. She was my sister."

Kimimela's eyes opened wide, and she gasped. "Michael! How terrible!"

"Mary Anne's mother told her at the same time. I guess my father told her to tell her."

"Did your mother know?"

"I don't see how she could not have known. Mary Anne's mother, Rosalee was her name, was in the house all day. There were four or five light-skinned slave children in the quarters. I had never thought much about Mary Anne's light skin."

"What happened to them?"

"My father freed them that same year. He said he had been thinking about it for a long time. He gave Rosalee a piece of land on the edge of the property to farm. We had two hundred sixty acres in tobacco and cotton. He gave her some pigs and a good mule and sent people over to help her with chores."

"What became of Mary Anne?" Kimimela said.

Michael stared at the stream. Kimimela turned to him, watching him struggle, wanting to hold him.

"I watched them as they left the quarters. Everything they owned was in the wagon. I had never thought about how little they owned. Mary Anne was sitting on some goods in the bed. She looked me straight in the eyes until they drove out of sight." He looked away until the pain subsided.

"I never saw her again. I was sent away to school in Richmond. We had been playmates and friends. Now I was the master's white son, and she was a Negro."

Kimimela looked up at him. "You keep saying it's a different world now, but it's not really different, is it?" she said.

He looked down at her and smiled thinly. "Change can be painfully slow, but it is coming. And it is a new world, for me at least. I have you."

She leaned back and frowned playfully. "You don't *have* me. I don't belong to you."

He smiled. They were quiet a long moment as they watched the ripples in the stream where fish had broken the surface briefly. A blue heron glided to the stream like a ghost, slowed with extended wings and settled without a sound in the shallows on the far side.

He spoke without looking at her. "You know, we might be cousins, you and I."

She turned abruptly toward him. "What do you mean, cousins!"

"There's a family legend that includes an Indian woman a long time ago. My family has been in Virginia since earliest settlement. We've not been able to confirm it, but every generation repeats the story."

"How do you feel about that, being part Indian?" she said. "If it is true."

"Good," he said. "Good. In the new world that is coming, we Indians will be able to control our affairs and our land. And our destiny." He smiled.

"Hah, I see! You will control nothing here, wasichu!" She hit him hard on his arm.

He recoiled. "Ouch!" He rubbed his arm. "You're violent!"

She smiled. "It is our way. Violence has always been part of the Beothuk way. But since the confederation was formed, maybe that will change. Raiding and warfare between tribes has almost ended. Now we recognize a common enemy." She touched his chest gently with her pointed finger. "You," she said.

"That's good," he said. "I mean that raiding and warfare have ended."

She sobered. "The elders worry," she said. "How will the young men earn status and show their bravery if they cannot count coup? How can they increase their wealth if they cannot steal horses?"

She picked up a pebble and threw it into the stream. "Not just men. Some women went on raids."

"Women?" he said. "That's not common, is it? They must be tough characters."

"No, it's not common. But some women enjoy raiding for the same reasons that men do." She lay back on the grassy bank.

"When I was a young girl and listened to the stories told by the raiders, I thought it would be exciting to go on raids. I went raiding when I was eleven. Grandfather didn't want me to go, so a friend, a boy my age, and I snuck away at night and caught up with a raiding party that had left about two hours before.

"The men in the raiding party thought it was funny. Some said to send me back to camp because Howahkan would be angry. But sneaking away to join a raiding party was what every boy, and some girls, did at an early age. It was part of growing up.

"So they let us stay. The boy was told to help the water-boy. I was to tend to the horses. These were important things to do, and we were proud.

"After they returned from the raid, they gave each of us some of the things they had taken at the Crow village. I got a mirror and a comb. They gave my friend a small axe."

"Was Howahkan angry when you returned?"

"The leader of the party walked me to Howahkan's tipi. When we entered the tipi, Grandfather was sitting before the cold fire pit. He didn't look up when we came in. After the leader and I sat down, he told Grandfather how brave I was, and he told about how I had been careful in tending the horses.

"Grandfather said nothing. The leader left, and Grandfather still stared at the cold fire. After a long time, he looked at me and said that he had been very worried. He had lost his only son, my father, and he didn't want to lose me. But then he congratulated me on my first raid and said that he was proud of me.

"Did you go raiding again?" he said.

"Two more times, but still as water-girl and tending the horses. I probably would have become a real raider, but my interests and ambitions changed." She pushed herself up into a sitting position.

"Do you regret the change that is coming?" he said.

"I will regret the loss of the old ways, most of them," she said. "I have not regretted the loss of war since the formation of the confederation. War was at the heart of Beothuk life. But it had to end if we were to survive. I think we can change the things we do without losing the values behind them."

"Kimi, change is going to sweep the plains in ways that we cannot imagine. You have told me how much the Beothuk and other tribes depend on the buffalo for many things: food, tipis, coverings, containers, religion. I heard at the Point that some people in Washington and at the Point are encouraging hide hunters to go to the plains to kill the buffalo. 'Kill the buffalo, and you've killed the Indian,' they say. It is not a happy thought. What would the People do if there were no buffalo?"

"I can't see an end to the buffalo," she said. "They are like the stars in the sky."

Michael thought that she said this wishfully, nervously.

"Come," he said. "Let's walk." He stood and reached for her hand. She brushed the hand aside playfully and stood on her own.

They strolled down the center of the lane. They passed a tipi that was made of well-weathered skins. Its side was painted with intricate geometrical designs and simple depictions of animals.

They walked on and stopped before another painted tipi. Michael studied the designs. One scene depicted a battle. There were mounted figures and some afoot. This was accompanied by what appeared to be heavenly bodies hovering above stick figures and an animal, perhaps a bear.

"Interesting," Michael said, still studying the painting. He turned to Kimimela.

"Paintings on tipis sometimes show important battles or hunting by the warrior who lives here," Kimimela said. "Sometimes it shows something about a dream or a vision quest. If the dreamer has had a vision, he talks about it with village wise men. Sometimes he has a skilled painter help him with the painting."

"Very interesting," Michael said.

They continued strolling down the lane. Michael stopped when they reached his tipi. He stared at the walls. The tipi was new, and the skins were unmarked.

"I have the newest tipi in the village," he said. "It's beautiful."

"Yes, I think so," she said. "I made it."

His eyes opened wide. "You did?"

"Women do all the work on tipis. They prepare the skins, sew them together and cut where necessary. They decide where the tipis will be set up, they set them up, and they take them down. They are responsible for the inside of the tipi. All men can do is paint the outside."

Michael looked again at his unblemished tipi wall. He looked at Kimimela. She saw the expectant look on his face.

"No," she said. "You cannot. Painting is not for decoration. It is to record something important that happened to the person who lives there. Have you done something that the people in this village will think is important? To you and those who live around you?"

He grimaced. "Well, since you put it that way, no. I have done nothing important enough to memorialize."

Kimimela looked puzzled. "I don't know that word, 'mem-or-ee-uh-lize'," she said slowly, imitating his pronunciation carefully.

"Since I cannot paint my tipi," he said, "I at least need some consolation."

"I don't know 'con-so-la-shun.' You're doing this on purpose."

"Come inside my tipi. I will explain." He pulled the flap aside for her to enter. He smiled.

She hesitated a moment. Then she smiled thinly, bent and entered. She had begun to understand the meaning of the word, "consolation."

# CHAPTER TWELVE

## My Ancestral Name Is Shanawdithit

The interior of the tipi was dark but for the bubble of soft light from the single candle and a small fire in the fire pit. A light rain pattered on the hide walls of the tipi.

Michael and Kimimela lay in his blankets. She was on her back. The blanket partially covered her, leaving her breasts exposed.

Michael was raised on an elbow, facing her, his hand supporting his head. He appeared to be in a trance, studying her small, perfect breasts. She noticed his stare, smiled and pulled the blanket to her chin.

He reached over and pulled the edge of the blanket down slowly to expose a breast. He leaned down and kissed the nipple. She giggled and raised the blanket again to her chin.

He kissed her lips and leaned back. "What does your name mean? Kimimela?"

"Kimimela wasn't my first name. My first name was Dowan-howee. It means Singing Voice. My father named me. He said I was always singing or shouting or talking. I never was quiet. Grandfather told me this. Grandfather changed my name to Kimimela when I was ten. It means Butterfly. He said Butterfly represents courage and is a symbol of change and freedom."

"He knew even then," Michael said, "when you were only ten."

"Yes, but he also said that I was always flying about, inspecting everything and looking at everything. He said that someday I would fly away from him, like a butterfly. I have told him many times that I would never do that. He gets sad when we talk about this.

"He has lost too many people. He lost his wife when she was young. She was Lakota, and he took a Lakota name in her honor. He must have loved her very much. He never talks about her."

Kimimela's eyes sparkled in the firelight. Michael leaned over and kissed her eyes. She smiled a sad smile and looked up at him. He kissed her lips.

"I have another name," she said. "My ancestral Beothuk name is Shanawdithit. My father gave me this name on my first day of life. Shanawdithit was a beloved leader of the Beothuk people long, long ago."

Michael stroked her cheek, spread his fingers and pushed his hand into her hair, pulling her head around to him. He kissed her lips, then leaned back.

"Tell me about the Beothuk," he said. "Not today, but about their beginnings, their history. Tell me what the old people say."

She looked up to the dark peak of the tipi.

"Long, long ago, we didn't live on these plains. We lived far, far east of here, on an island in the cold sea. We hunted and fished and lived at peace with our neighbors. Have you ever heard Indian people called 'Red Indians'?"

"Sure, it's a common expression," he said.

"We were the first Red Indians. We used to rub our bodies with red earth. Not just our bodies. Also clothing and weapons and things we used. And our tipis. Well, they were not tipis. They were shaped like tipis, but covered with bark instead of hides. They were called mamateeks. That is what the old men say.

"We lived at peace, with the land and the four-leggeds. Then the white men came. Many people were killed by the Strangers—we called the whites 'Strangers'—and we were dying from their diseases. They took our game and our land and gave guns to our enemies to fight us. That's when the elders decided that we must leave our island in the cold sea. We kept moving west over many, many winters, and here we are.

"Shanawdithit stayed behind. When the Strangers questioned her, she said that all of the Beothuk people were gone widdun. Gone, dead. So the Strangers would not look for us. She saved the people. This is what the old men say."

She stared into the darkness at the peak of the tipi. Michael watched her.

After a long moment, he asked, "Have the Beothuk always been allied with the Lakota?"

"When we settled on the plains long, long ago, we were welcomed by the Lakota. We learned much from them, and they learned from us. We have intermarried for many generations. Now, when the old men tell us about our past, sometimes I don't know whether they are talking about our Beothuk past or our Lakota past.

"But some things are not confusing. I know the names of some of my Beothuk ancestors. Doochebewshet, Shendoreth, Ewinon. I know nothing about them, but I want to know. I really want to know. The old men tell us that as long as we remember the names, we can sing them back from the spirit world. Sometimes, at night, when I am alone, I can see them, but they are only shadows. I speak to them, trying to sing them to me, trying to get them to step into the light and talk to me, but they never do." Michael leaned back and looked into her eyes. He wiped a tear from her cheek.

He lifted the bone pendant that hung loosely on its plaited leather thong around her neck. The pendant was about four inches long, flat and well-polished. The rawhide thong was laced through a hole at the top. The bottom of the pendant was splayed out like the tail of a swallow. Long lines had been carved or scratched along the edges. Ladderlike images projected out from the long grooves. Carved geometric designs filled the spaces between the lines.

"This is beautiful. Tell me about it," he said. "I have never seen you without it."

She took the pendant from him and held it in both hands. "It is the most important thing I own. It was given to me by my grandfather after my, um, Ishna Ta Awi Cha Lowan ceremony. It's when a girl has had her first, um, um, bleeding. This ceremony says that she is no longer a child and is becoming a woman."

"I can confirm that you are a woman," he said. He touched her cheek lightly. She smiled.

"Is it Beothuk?" he said.

"Yes, it is very old. It belonged to grandfather's grandmother. He said that it was made by an ancestor who lived on the island in the cold sea. He said that it would give me good fortune and keep me safe from harm."

They fell silent. She snuggled close to him and pulled the blanket over her shoulders. He slid down beside her, his face buried in her hair.

He pondered a long moment. Then he leaned back and rose on an elbow. He spoke softly. "Why have you not married?"

She rolled over on her back. She looked up at him, then at the peak of the tipi. "Grandfather has mentioned men, but he said I could decide."

"That's not . . . usual, is it?" he said.

"No." She laughed lightly. "One man from another village offered a hundred horses."

Michael grinned. "That must be a record," he said. "Howahkan must have tried to persuade you to accept."

"He did try, but I didn't like that man." Michael waited. She turned to face him.

"I was married once," she said. "In a painting."

Michael frowned. "What do you mean?"

"An American painter made a drawing of me and a trapper. Last year. Do you understand trapper?"

"Yes," he said.

"The painter said he was going to paint a trapper taking an Indian bride. He only did a drawing. He said he would finish it at his home in the east. I liked the drawing. I wish I could see the painting."

"Who was the trapper?" he said.

"I don't know," she said. "He was with the painter and a man from Europe who said he wanted to see the wild country. I didn't know our country was wild."

Michael smiled. "Yes, it is a wild country filled with wild people. Especially the women." He stroked her cheek. "Did you ever see them again?"

"Only the trapper. He came back by himself and asked grandfather for my hand. He offered a hundred horses and a hundred beaver skins."

"Your grandfather must have been very tempted."

"He was," she said. "But the trapper smelled bad."

Michael smiled. He leaned over and kissed her lips. "I'm glad."

"Aren't most Beothuk girls married by . . . by—"

"By my age?" she said lightly.

"Well, yes," he said.

"Yes, they are. Some as early as thirteen, fourteen, fifteen years old. There has been some pressure. No one says anything to me, but it is there." She absentmindedly rolled the edge of the blanket, then unrolled it.

"Have you heard of the four virtues, the four things that the Beothuk think most important?" she said.

"No," he said.

"Strength of mind. Fortitude, I think you would say. Generosity. Wisdom. And childbearing." She looked down, then glanced up at him and down again. "Do you understand?"

"Yes, I do," he said.

"They know I am different. When I was a young girl, I learned quilling and beading and other things that Beothuk women are expected to know, but when I became more interested in learning and schooling, I did less of the traditional things. People thought I was a little strange, and they didn't like it, but grandfather said I could do as I wished.

"And they know now that grandfather's vision of the future includes change. But most think that the woman's role in Beothuk life does not change. We lose too many babies at birth and to sickness and too many people in war." She looked into the black void at the top of the tipi. "It is hard."

The rain increased in intensity, making a staccato sound on the skin walls of the tipi. Michael and Kimimela looked at the dark walls and listened to the rain.

"Where did you learn Spanish?" Michael said.

"I went to university in Mexico City," she said.

He frowned. "There's a university in Mexico City?"

She rolled over to face him, pity on her face. "Poor Michael. There was a university in Mexico City when your Pilgrims were starving." She leaned over and kissed him.

"Our Pilgrims . . . how . . ." He didn't know how to continue.

"What did you do . . . what did you study in Mexico City? How long were you there?" he said.

"Almost two years. I studied history mostly. And other things," she said.

"Not Spanish?"

"No. I learned Spanish at the convent where I stayed," she said, "and at the Bank of Pity."

"The Bank of Pity?"

"Nacional Monte de Piedad. The people called it the Bank of Pity. You call it a pawnshop. It's where Mexicans take things to pawn for money. Jewels, clothes, tools, religious things, art, anything. I loved to go there. I bought things I needed, and I talked and talked. I learned Spanish, and I taught the workers some Beothuk. They loved it."

"Mexicans speaking Beothuk," Michael mumbled and shook his head.

"What did you say?" she said.

"Nothing." He leaned over and kissed her lips. He caressed her breasts under the blanket.

"I went to school in your country too," she said.

He recoiled. "What! In my country? When? Where?"

"When I was a young girl. Two years. In Pennsylvania. The school did not want to accept me, but grandfather paid so much, they let me in. I didn't like the cooking, sewing and housemaking. I wanted to study with the boys, but they wouldn't do that, so they set up a separate plan for me. I persuaded them to let two American girls study with me. The school didn't like all this, but they wanted the gold.

"They tried to cut my braids, but I refused. They were so angry. They would have been angrier if they had known that I was teaching the American girls Beothuk." She smiled wickedly.

Michael was dumbfounded. He shook his head. He wondered whether this girl would ever seem ordinary to him. "Your parents must have missed you," he said.

She rolled over and stared at the dark peak. "I had no parents. Your soldiers killed them when I was five. I remember them."

He reached over and touched her cheek. "Not my soldiers, Kimi. That was another time, another world."

She rolled back to face him. Her cheeks glistened in the soft candlelight. He pulled her to him and held her tightly. He leaned back and kissed her lips and her wet cheek. He rolled over to lie on his back. He stared into the darkness at the peak.

They were quiet and still. The rain pattered on the tipi wall. She thought he must be sleeping and turned to look at him. His eyes were open, staring into the black void at the peak.

"Michael?" she said.

After a long moment, he rolled over to face her. "I know how it feels to lose parents. My mother and father died when I was at West Point. Yellow fever. It was an epidemic, killed my uncle, my aunt, two cousins, all my relations. I have no one. Except Mary Anne."

Kimimela reached across his chest and held him. He raised her chin and kissed her lips. He leaned back and rose on an elbow.

"Tell me a story," he said. "A Beothuk story."

She pulled away from him and lay on her back. She crossed her arms on her chest.

A Beothuk story, she pondered. She had never told a story. She had never been asked to tell a story. Telling stories was what old men did around the fire and mothers did for their children.

She looked at the black peak, through the smoke hole, into the darkness of the spirit world to a bright land.

She frowned, pursed her lips, and began. "One day, long ago, Raven was very hungry. Her mother and father and all her family, and all of the people of her village were starving. Raven flew a great distance looking for food. Then she saw Salmon below, lying in the shallows. She flew down to him.

"Salmon said to Raven, 'I am dying, Raven. I know you are hungry. I give myself to your people.' Raven thanked Salmon and honored him with nechwa, bark tobacco. When Salmon's spirit had departed, Raven tried to drag him, to take him to the hungry people. But Salmon was too big, and Raven was too weak. She could not move him.

"Then Raven looked up and saw Caribou lying at the edge of a wood. She went to him. Caribou said, 'Raven, I am dying. I know you and your people are hungry. I give myself to you.' Raven thanked him and honored him with nechwa.

"Raven knew she could not move Caribou, so she decided to leave Caribou and Salmon and fly to her village. She would bring the hungry people to Salmon and Caribou so they could have plenty to eat. But Raven was so hungry, she did not have the strength to fly.

" 'I will just eat a little so I will have the strength to fly,' she said to herself. So she ate. And ate. And ate. Until her belly was swollen, and she could not fly. 'I will just sleep a little,' she said to herself. 'Then I will be able to fly.'

"When she awakened, she was hungry again. She had to have the strength to fly, so she ate. And ate. And ate. Until her belly was swollen, and she could not fly. She slept. She kept doing this again and again until only the bones of Salmon and Caribou remained.

"Raven flew back to her village. She was ashamed, but she tried to hide her shame. 'I have found bones of Salmon and Caribou! Let's go there and pick them!' But no one answered. They were all dead. Raven was left alone with her swollen belly."

Kimimela looked at Michael. His eyes were closed. She rolled over and snuggled against him.

The rain had ended, and the dark clouds had moved away, revealing a cold moon. The moonlight illuminated shapes and cast shadows.

A dark figure leaned against the massive trunk of a large bur oak across the lane from Michael's tipi. The silhouette of the figure was a black shadow that merged with the dark outline of the trunk. The shadow saw the flap of Michael's tent open and move slowly aside. The shadow leaned forward and in the moonlight became Olaktay.

A bending figure stepped from the tipi opening and stood upright. Olaktay withdrew into the foliage and watched. The moonlight illuminated Kimimela's face. She leaned back into the opening, as if to say something or look at something. Then she straightened, turned and walked up the lane toward her tipi. Olaktay stepped from his hiding place and watched her.

# CHAPTER THIRTEEN

## Brothers and Sisters Together

Michael and Kimimela stood beside the trail at the perimeter of the village. Their horses were tied nearby to tree limbs. He wore his full uniform. The wool shell jacket adorned with the plain shoulder straps of his second lieutenant rank was buttoned from the tight bottom to the top at the high collar. The wool trousers chafed in the heat, and the billed forage cap lay on his head like a griddle. He lamented anew his decision not to bring his cotton field service uniform to the village.

He shifted his weight from right foot to left and back again. Pulling at the collar, he rubbed the sweat that rolled down his temples with his hand. He removed his cap and pulled a bandanna from his pocket. He wiped his head and face vigorously, then replaced the hat and stuffed the bandanna into his pocket.

"Damn, I have never been so uncomfortable," he said. "I find it hard to believe that I could ever have been comfortable in this outfit. When are these people going to get here?"

The coded message from Major Burke had told little. A Methodist minister from an eastern philanthropic organization wished to spend a month at the village to determine whether the Beothuk would be receptive to a Christian mission settling among them. Washington had approved the visit.

Michael shook his head in disgust. Ill-advised and bad timing. Does Washington know what is going on out here? On the other hand, he mused, maybe conflict could be avoided, for a time at least, if Washington thought the Indians could be influenced by something other than violence.

Michael paced. He pulled the bandanna from his pocket and wiped his face again.

Kimimela smiled. "The scout said they had passed the second spring. That means, about, well, twenty minutes of your time from the spring to here. So they should be just about. . . there!" She pointed.

He looked up the slight incline to the height where the trail began the descent to the village. A party of riders moved across the crest. The Beothuk guide was followed by two Americans in black suits. Damn, thought Michael, they must be roasting.

An escort of four warriors followed at the rear of the party. An army enlisted man in uniform rode beside the escort. The soldier chattered and gestured to the warriors.

The party moved down the trail toward Michael and Kimimela. Michael, at once the official representative of the United States frontier army, straightened and stepped onto the trail.

The party reined in before him. One of the black suits dismounted slowly. He straightened and flexed his back.

"Welcome to the main village of The People. I'm Lieutenant Michael Wagner. I think Major Burke has explained my presence here."

Reverend William John Wesley Throckmorton thrust

his hand toward Michael. Michael took his hand, and the Reverend shook hands vigorously. "He did, indeed," Throckmorton said, sighing heavily. "I am glad to see you and the end of this blessed ride. I am not a horseman."

Reverend Throckmorton was not only not a horseman, he was not a westerner. Tall, square-jawed and clean-shaven, he was a Maryland minister who was a leading light in a new organization that called itself Brothers and Sisters Together.

This body, only two years old and growing daily in membership and influence, had dedicated itself to improving the condition of the American Indian.

Another name had been suggested for the fledgling organization: Friends of the Indian. But this title was rejected as too bland, too ambiguous, too condescending, even self-serving, as if the organization were all about the members and not about the Indians. The founders selected the present name as all-encompassing. We are all brothers and sisters in the family of God, they agreed. So they dedicated themselves to bringing their red brothers and sisters into this saintly family. Reverend Throckmorton and his son were the first members of the body to venture into the wild western garden.

The Reverend Throckmorton, as one of the founders of Brothers and Sisters Together, perhaps had thrust himself into the forefront of the western effort, but the other leaders had readily agreed to the assignment. They knew about his history. He had told them more than once. He had been dedicated at birth by his father, a Methodist minister, to God and His work. He had not disappointed. As a child, he had been single-minded in his play and his education. As an adult and minister, he glorified God and worked diligently to bring sinners into His fold.

Following the family tradition, the Reverend Throckmorton had dedicated his son to the ministry at birth. At nineteen years, the son was now his father's right hand and his apprentice.

The Reverend gestured toward his son who sat slumped in his saddle. He was clearly exhausted. "This is my son, John Wesley." Michael nodded to him. John Wesley smiled weakly and raised a hand in greeting.

Throckmorton gestured toward the corporal. "Major Burke kindly lent Corporal McGill to us to act as interpreter." The corporal smiled and saluted casually. Michael frowned and returned the salute.

"We'll talk in the village, Corporal," Michael said.

"Yes, sir," Rufus said in a manner as casual as his salute.

Michael turned back to the Reverend, then toward Kimimela. "This is Kimimela. She is the headman's granddaughter and his chief advisor. Any questions you have related to the village, see her. Any questions related to your purpose here, see me. A tipi has been set up for your use. After you have rested, we'll talk."

The Reverend smiled and nodded.

Michael and Kimimela walked to their horses, untied the reins and mounted. They walked their mounts onto the trail and turned toward the village. The Reverend mounted slowly, as if he feared that a quick movement would break something, and the party fell in behind Michael and Kimimela.

Michael and Corporal Rufus McGill sat on benches on opposite sides of an arbor table. Rufus slouched on the bench and leaned on the table.

"This is sure nice. Like no other Beothuk village I ever seen," Rufus said. "Things sure are changin'."

"They are indeed," Michael said. "Where did you learn your Beothuk?"

"My grandma was Beothuk. After my grandpa died, she came to live with me and my ma. Didn't speak more'n a few words 'uv English, so she and my ma spoke only Beothuk. When she came to live with us, I was a little kid, so I picked it up fast."

"When I growed up, I done some tradin' with the Beothuks, and my Beothuk improved pretty fast. Visited a few army posts during my tradin' days, and the army decided they wanted me to interpret for 'em. I said I would, but I had uh understandin' with 'em. I told 'em I'm an interpreter, not a fighter. They said okay and give me my corporal's stripes the first day.

"And here I set. I don't drill, and I don't shoot. I bet I hadn't shot twenty rounds in two years. And that's fine with me."

"Hmm. Good arrangement." Michael smiled. "On that point, Corporal, we will dispense with army routine as long as you're here. Best to be as invisible as possible. The United States army isn't terribly well liked here. In fact, you can fold the uniform, if you wish, and find some other clothes. And you'll not tell tales if you see me out of uniform. Are we okay on that point?"

Rufus smiled conspiratorially. "I can sure agree on that, Lieutenant," Rufus said. "Fine with me."

The Reverend Throckmorton held forth in the enlarged arbor. A framework of branches and cut saplings had been laced together to extend the arbor to cover space that would seat two hundred shoulder-to-shoulder spectators. There were never so many in attendance. The more usual number was fifteen or twenty. Some would appear at the announced hour. Some would wander in, stay a while, and leave at any moment.

Rufus gave a rather literal translation, sometimes elaborating to try to make sense of the Reverend's scholarly delivery. Generally the members of the audience were bored or unimpressed or confused. Rufus tried hard to appear interested in what he was doing, but he could not always avoid reflecting the boredom of the listeners.

On one notable afternoon, all this changed. The arbor was packed. The Reverend had announced that he was going to talk about the beginning of the world. People had arrived early, sitting as close to the front as possible. Many stood around the perimeter of the seated congregation. There was a hum of excited conversation.

The Reverend Throckmorton was thrilled. He had finally found a topic that would reach these beloved heathen. He smiled benevolently and held up his arms to quiet the chattering. The hum declined to silence. All looked intently at the Reverend.

He began. He opened his worn Bible to the first page of text and read: "In the beginning, God created the heaven and the earth." He paused as Rufus interpreted. "And the earth was without form, and void. And darkness was upon the face of the deep. And the spirit of God moved upon the face of the waters.

"And God said, let there be light, and there was light. And God saw the light, that it was good. And God divided the light from the darkness. And God called the light Day, and the darkness he called Night. And the evening and the morning were the first day."

As quickly as the Reverend paused, members of the audience looked immediately from him to Rufus. They leaned forward, some cupping their ears, and listened intently to the translation. Then they looked at each other, puzzled. A murmuring rose from all sides. The Reverend was elated. *The people are moved by the story of the creation!*

He continued: "And God said, let there be a firmament in the midst of the waters, and let it divide the waters from the waters. And God made the firmament, and divided the waters, which were above the firmament, and it was so. And God called the firmament Heaven. And the evening and the morning were the second day."

As Rufus translated, the murmuring increased in intensity. The people looked from neighbor to neighbor and chattered louder and louder. Some raised their arms and shouted.

The Reverend was ecstatic. *The people are excited!* He raised his voice to be heard over the din. He shouted: "And God said, let the waters under the heaven be gathered together unto one place, and let the dry land appear, and it was so. And God called the dry land earth, and the gathering together of the waters called the Seas, and God saw that it was good."

The people turned in unison to look at Rufus. They leaned forward and listened in silence. When he was finished, the people jumped up. They shouted and jostled and churned. The Reverend was beside himself. *God be praised!*

The shouts and murmuring subsided and ended as the people turned and walked slowly from the arbor.

The Reverend stopped, open-mouthed. *What is happening? Where are they going? The lesson is not finished!*

The arbor was empty, but for the Reverend and Rufus. And Kimimela and Michael who stood at the edge of the arbor. They had walked over when they saw the congregation leaving. Kimimela and Michael walked to the front where Throckmorton still stood, slumped, before the empty tabernacle. Throckmorton turned to Michael and Kimimela. The Reverend appeared to be on the point of collapse.

"What happened?" he said in a pained voice.

Kimimela forced a smile, a smile of sympathy. She said softly. "Reverend Throckmorton, the people did not come to your meeting to learn how the world was created. They know how the world was created. They came to hear you, an American holy man, talk about it."

Throckmorton was drained. "But . . . but this is the story of the creation."

"Not if you are Beothuk," Kimimela said.

Throckmorton stared, open-mouthed.

"Sit down, Reverend. Please," Kimimela said softly. Throckmorton turned around, found the bench behind him and slowly sat down.

Michael touched Kimimela's arm. "Kimimela, do you think—"

Kimimela glanced at Michael and frowned. She turned back to the Reverend and sat beside him on the bench.

She began. "In the beginning, the Beothuk lived inside the earth. They saw a hole that led to the surface of the earth, and they went through it. All left except one person who stayed behind.

"The people liked this land. It was light and warm, and it provided all the food they needed. They were happy, and they decided to stay.

"But the good times ended. There was a bad drought, and food became scarce. The people suffered, and many died. The person who had stayed in the earth saw all this and was sad. This person wanted to help the people, so this last person came through the hole and became Deer.

The people were saved, and thereafter Deer had a special place in Beothuk life."

Throckmorton looked blankly at her. He waited for more, but Kimimela said nothing.

"That's it?" he said.

"There are other stories of the beginning," she said, "but some are very complicated. I'm not sure I understand sometimes."

"It's very simplistic," the Reverend said. "People living under the ground?"

"God created day and night?" she said.

"The people came through a hole to the surface of the earth?" he said, as if to a child.

"God created the land and the seas?"

"The last person became a deer?" he said.

"God created man, and he created woman from one of the man's ribs?" she said.

"Kimi," Michael said. She looked at him blankly, then at Throckmorton. It was a look of sadness, or pity.

The Reverend still held the open Bible on his lap. He looked at it and closed it slowly and deliberately. He looked at Kimimela. "The Christian believes on faith what he cannot know by experience," Throckmorton said softly with all the energy he could muster.

Michael watched Kimimela, then turned to the Reverend. Michael sighed. "So do the heathen, Reverend. So do the heathen."

Throckmorton stood slowly, his bones and muscles protesting the effort. He faced the empty tabernacle and spoke softly, as if to a congregation: "The lesson for tomorrow shall be Redemption."

He turned to Michael and Kimimela. "Until then," he said. He smiled weakly and walked slowly toward the lane.

# CHAPTER FOURTEEN

## Michael Learns to Dance

"I'll make a fool of myself," Michael said.

"No," said Kimimela, "just follow the other boys."

They stood on the path that looked over the bathing spot below the village. They watched six naked children splash and jump in the shallows, striking the surface with flat palms, sending up fountains of spray. They giggled and laughed loudly.

"Yeah, boys," Michael said. "I'm not a boy."

"Same for me. But I don't care. I haven't done the Evening Dance since I was a young girl, and I want to do it again. If you won't do it with me, I'll choose someone else." She lifted her chin in defiance, a gesture he had seen more than once from her.

He frowned. Was she challenging him or threatening him? Or playing with him? "All right, but I'll make a fool of myself. I never liked dancing. Any kind of dancing."

The temperature had dropped only slightly since sundown, and the sides of the large tipi were rolled up to admit cooling breezes. The rolled sides also permitted onlookers crowded outside to view the event.

The interior of the tipi was crowded with eager participants. The half dozen girls, fifteen to eighteen years old, except Kimimela, sat on the ground in a line on the south side of the fire pit where flames crackled brightly. Steam rose from two pots that lay in the embers.

Six boys, including Michael, were aligned on the north side. Michael sat at the end of the line, away from the door, feeling very foolish. He was dressed in fine deerskin trousers and shirt that Kimimela had made for him. She had helped him paint his face and tie his sash with its dangling deer hooves that tinkled when he walked.

On the west side of the tipi, a girl and a boy whom the men had chosen to act as honorary chaperones sat stiffly, cognizant of their position, which carried some prestige and few duties. Beside them sat two other boys who were to act as servers.

Singers sat on the north side of the entrance near the boys. They sang and drummed as the participants found their places and settled down.

Michael looked at Kimimela who sat in the middle of the row of girls. She wore her best dress of decorated soft deerskin. She looked straight ahead, as if she were studying the tipi wall opposite. Her face was a mask, serious, thoughtful.

When all of the players and guests had settled in their places, the girls stood and walked over to the boys. Each girl chose a partner by kicking the sole of his moccasin. Kimimela kicked Michael's foot with more force than the others. He resisted the impulse to smile.

The boys rose and formed a line, each boy on the left side of the girl who had chosen him. The singing and drumming began again. Each dancer grasped his or her partner's belt, and all sidestepped, rocking gently with bent knees, clockwise around the fire.

Michael watched the boy nearest him and imitated him. He looked back at Kimimela and smiled ever so slightly, but sobered when he saw her serious face.

He winced when he stepped on the foot of the girl beside him. He lost the rhythm, shuffled when he should have been dipping and got thoroughly confused. Kimimela frowned at him and grasped his belt tighter. Gradually she led him back to the proper cadence and rhythm. He swayed when he should sway and dipped when he should dip. A brief flicker of a smile on Kimimela's face reassured him.

After dancing several minutes, Michael was beginning to think he had it. Then the music stopped. He looked around, released his hold on Kimimela and turned to take his seat. Kimimela held his belt tightly and pulled him back. She scowled and bent close to his ear. She whispered sternly, "Watch!"

He glanced right and left. None of the other dancers had moved from their place. The music began again, and the same dance commenced. Michael surprised himself with his dexterity. He was beginning to enjoy this, but the music stopped again. The dancers disengaged and sat down in their segregated lines. Michael looked at Kimimela. She glanced at him and nodded slightly. He relaxed. Maybe he had passed the test.

After a short rest, the music started again. The boys rose, Michael following suit, and walked to the girls' line where each boy would choose a partner. Michael stopped in front of the young girl on Kimimela's left side and leaned forward. The girl shrank and looked wide-eyed at Kimimela.

Michael straightened and stepped over to Kimimela. She scowled at him and stood. They moved in the rhythmic rocking two-step gait once again. Michael began to feel the hypnotic effect of the drums and the dance.

They danced and danced. Michael began to feel lightheaded, like he had just finished his third glass of wine. He stared into Kimimela's eyes and felt that he must reach for her.

The music ended. The dancers all around him dropped their hands, turned around as if hypnotized and retreated to their seats. Michael and Kimimela stood transfixed. They still held each other's belt and looked into each other's eyes. They leaned toward each other. They stopped, looked around and realized that they stood alone in the center of the tipi. Everyone stared at them. They dropped their hands and returned quickly to their seats. Kimimela stared into the fire.

The music began again. Nobody moved. Michael looked at Kimimela. He followed her gaze and noticed that everyone looked toward the chaperones and servers. The two servers picked up wooden bowls. They stood and walked to the steaming kettles. Each dipped his bowl in a kettle and swished it around. One righted his bowl, and Michael strained to see what it held. He saw a chunk of meat. The other swished the bowl again and brought it up. When he turned in Michael's direction, Michael was stunned when he saw that the bowl contained a puppy's head.

The servers danced to the center of the girls' line. They swayed and dipped in front of Kimimela and the girl on her left.

*No, Kimi, please, no.*

One of the servers gave Kimimela his bowl, and the other server offered his bowl to the girl beside her. The servers' backs were to the boys, and Michael could not see which bowl was offered to Kimimela. Kimimela and the other girl rose and danced to the boys' line. The girl kicked her partner's foot, and Kimimela kicked Michael's foot. Then they danced back to their side.

Following the boy's lead, Michael stood and danced beside him toward the girls. As they approached, the girls offered the bowls to the boys. But when they reached for the bowls, the girls pulled them back. But not before Michael saw with great relief that Kimimela's bowl contained the chunk of meat and not the head. He pursed his lips, trying to communicate his thanks to her without speaking, but she looked blankly at him. The girls did this four times, and on the fourth attempt, the girls gave the bowls to the boys.

The servers then filled bowls and danced to the boys' line. When all of the boys had received their bowls, they stood and danced to the girls' line where they performed the same offer and withdrawal routine. On the fourth offer, the boys gave the girls the bowls.

The servers danced back to the pot, filled bowls and distributed them to the boys. Boys and girls ate silently. Michael stole a glance at Kimimela, but she did not look up from her bowl.

When all had finished eating, the bowls were collected. The singing and drumming began again, and the dancing followed. Michael felt at one with the others now, with no coaching and no imitation. The lightheadedness returned, and he felt himself drifting, flowing with the music and the movement of the dance.

But he longed to be alone with Kimimela. He danced closer to her than did the boys with their partners. He didn't care whether anyone noticed. He was alone with her in the tipi, alone with her in the universe. She was content to dance close to him, but she gave no sign that she was ready for the dance to end. She appeared transported to another dimension.

The hours wore on, and the dancers appeared to be in a trance, swaying and dipping, flowing forward, backward, sideways.

Then it ended. The chaperones stood and danced among the others to the tipi opening and went out. This was the signal that the dance was over. The drumming and singing stopped. The dancers stopped and filed out.

Michael and Kimimela walked out together. He turned to her to talk, but she looked straight ahead, silent, her face a mask. They walked silently down the lane toward his tipi. Others who walked on the lane veered off toward their tipis and were swallowed by the darkness.

They continued walking until they stood before his tipi.

Kimimela looked around. They were alone. She stopped, looked at him, then doubled over laughing.

"What?" he said.

"He offered me the puppy head! I started to take it to see what you would do." She laughed and doubled over again.

He frowned. "Kimi," he said, "I would have thrashed you. I have happily adopted many of your customs, but at eating puppy heads, I draw the line."

"You were so good!" she said. "Like you had done the Evening Dance all your life!"

He reached for her and pulled her to him. He looked into her eyes. "I will dance with you to the stars and beyond." He took her face in his hands and kissed her lips gently.

"I love you, Kimi."

She sobered. "Don't say that."

"But—"

"Go inside," she said. "Show me."

Kimimela and Howahkan faced each other across the cold fire pit in Howahkan's tipi. Contrary to what might be expected in a tipi of a warrior who lived alone, the interior was neat and well ordered. Since his wife, Kimimela's grandmother, died seven years ago, Kimimela had assumed responsibility for its care.

Howahkan stared into the empty fire pit. Kimimela watched him, waiting, wondering why he had asked her to sit with him this day.

He raised his head and looked at her. "Kimimela. You are a grown woman. Since you were a child, you have been responsible and wise. I realized early that you were different, that you wanted to experience new things and do new things, and I encouraged you to choose your own path. You know that, don't you?"

"Yes, Grandfather," she said.

"I have never forbidden anything you wished to do and have never forced anything on you. I have only counseled."

He paused. Kimimela waited, apprehensive.

"I will counsel again," he said. "You have become more than a teacher of Beothuk ways to Ambassador Michael."

She leaned forward. "But Grandfather—"

He raised a hand to silence her. "I do not condemn. I do not forbid. You will choose your path." He lowered his hand to his lap. "But know this. Ambassador Michael will leave this village. He will not take you with him. He may take your heart, but he will not take you."

He paused and looked at her, lovingly and compassionately. "I have seen this before. When the white man goes away, the Beothuk woman is left with nothing but shame. Even when the

white man has taken her with him, her life has been empty. She is no longer Beothuk, and she is not white. She has no roots and no spirit."

Kimimela stared into the cold fire pit. She felt its chill seeping into her body.

"Ambassador Michael is a good man. But he is an American. A soldier. A white man. A wasichu."

Kimimela's shoulders slumped. A tear rolled down her cheek.

"Kimimela. I only counsel. I know what I have seen. I cannot see what is to come. I tell the people about the world changing and how we must change with it. How it will change, I do not know. You will know better than I how we must live in the new world."

She raised her head and managed a slight smile. "Thank you, Grandfather."

He nodded. "Think on what I have said."

"I will, Grandfather."

# CHAPTER FIFTEEN

### John Wesley Glimpses Paradise

Michael stood in front of his tipi. He wore his army trousers, an Indian shirt and moccasins. He stretched and looked around. Everything sparkled from last night's rain. He turned toward the morning sun. He closed his eyes and felt his face warming under the soft rays of this midspring morning.

"Michael!"

He was startled. He looked up the lane to see Kimimela running toward him.

"Michael! Get ready! We leave now!"

He frowned. "Leave? Where?"

"A long trip, many days!" she said. "Come to the kiva. Quickly!"

She turned and ran toward her tipi. Michael watched her go, bewildered.

A large group of people stood near the kiva. Fifty warriors talked among themselves in hushed voices. They fussed over their horses, adjusting girths and other fittings. Villagers crowded around the group. Women, children and men mingled with the warriors, helping and chatting and laughing. The air was heavy with excitement and anticipation.

Twenty packhorses stood nearby, shifting their weight from right to left and back again. Handlers adjusted packsaddles and checked girths. Most of the panniers of stiff buffalo hide were empty. The others were only partially filled.

Howahkan talked with Kimimela. Michael walked up to them. Howahkan nodded to Michael and walked over to the packhorses. He spoke to the handlers who crowded in close to listen to him. Kimimela looked Michael up and down. She smiled. He wore all Indian clothing.

Howahkan untied his horse from the hitching rail and mounted. He spoke loudly for all to hear. "Mount! We are leaving!"

Warriors said their goodbyes to family and villagers. The tone was festive, and the conversational din mounted.

Kimimela and Michael walked to the rail where their horses were tied. She held the bandanna in her hand. "I'm sorry," she said.

"It's okay," Michael said. "I'll be in the dark with you."

She smiled. She folded the cloth into a blindfold and wrapped it around his head, covering his eyes.

"Where are we going?" he said. She tightened the bandanna and tied it.

"To meet the Celestials."

Howahkan's party rode in a scattered formation across a broad plain. Howahkan, Kimimela and Michael rode at the front. Warriors rode in twos and threes, in line or spreading out, finding their own paths.

The pack animals at the back stretched out in a neat line. The first animal was closely controlled by a warrior who held the horse's lead. The second packhorse was similarly led by a second warrior. The panniers of the two horses were not tightly packed, but the impressions on the packs revealed heavy contents. The other packhorses that followed were almost frisky with their light or empty panniers. These were tied together in twos or threes in a line, with the lead horse led by a handler.

The only sounds were the creaking of horse gear and the wind blowing through the tall grasses. A distant meadowlark called repeatedly.

Young John Wesley was shy to the point that some people thought him slow-witted. This was not the case at all. He was in fact a bright young man. His capability and intelligence were best displayed when he took on the mantle of teacher.

On this warm day, he stood in the arbor before a group of fifteen children and young people, from seven to seventeen years old, seated on the ground. This was the usual number at the mid-afternoon gathering. John Wesley had the services of Rufus since the interpreter assisted the Reverend only at his morning service.

John Wesley talked about Jesus and the feeding of the five thousand, the miracle of the five loaves and two fish. He thought the lesson would be appropriate for a people who always had to struggle to find food. He would show with this story that God watches over His children and provides for them.

Each time he waited for Rufus's translation, he looked over his flock and found himself returning time and time again to a particular member of the small congregation. Walika was a pretty seventeen-year-old with large, black eyes and soft lips that curved up slightly at the corners.

She wore a simple dress of elk skins, lightly decorated with colored quills and glass beads. She listened intently to John Wesley. Her eyes never left him.

Every time he looked at her, they made eye contact, and he was loath to break away. Now as he looked down at her, a hint of a smile played about her lips. Tiny dimples appeared briefly when she smiled. He shuddered. He hoped the heat in his cheeks was not visible.

When the lesson was finished, and the group stood to go their separate ways, Walika and three girlfriends walked by him, chattering. Walika brushed against him, smiled and walked away with her companions, laughing and gesturing.

John Wesley gathered his papers and a colored drawing of Jesus and the multitude and pushed them into a large envelope.

Rufus strolled over. "Pretty hard subject. Hope I got it right."

"I'm sure you did fine." John Wesley smiled. He straightened and pulled a bandanna from his pocket. He wiped his face and head. "Hot today."

"Sure is," Rufus said. "You oughta take a dip in the stream. Nice and cool. Least, that's what I heard the girls say just now. They're heading that way." Rufus grinned and pointed toward the bathing area at the foot of the village.

"Hmm, I may try it someday," John Wesley said. He turned to go. "Till tomorrow?" He nodded to Rufus who touched a finger to his hat brim. They walked their separate ways.

John Wesley walked slowly on a path downstream from the arbor. The bathing spot was a broad pool with a sandy bottom and a small sand landing. It was hidden from the trail by a heavy growth of rushes and sedges and a dense willow thicket. A couple of tall cottonwoods shaded the site to midstream.

John Wesley heard squeals and laughter ahead. He drew closer and heard splashing. He stepped off the trail into the thicket. He carefully moved branches aside, moving farther into the brush, until he was at the edge of the thicket. He slowly parted the bushes to a narrow opening through which he could see the stream.

He saw Walika, another girl her age and a third girl a couple of years younger, splashing and jumping up and down. They crouched in the shallow stream, and they stood to splash each other.

John Wesley was paralyzed. The girls were naked. He had had no experience with women. He had never seen a naked female body. He felt dizzy, and his vision blurred.

Walika squatted and sat down on the bottom, only her head and shoulders above the water. She scooped up a handful of sand and rubbed it on her arms and shoulders. A movement in the streamside foliage caught her eye. She looked intently at the spot. The brush parted slowly to reveal John Wesley's face. She saw him and smiled broadly.

"John Wesley!" she shouted. The opening in the brush closed immediately. The other girls were startled by her cry. The three girls crouched in the shallows until they were immersed up to their chins.

The others followed her gaze. "Where is he?" one of the girls said.

"John Wesley?" Walika called. He slowly parted the brush to reveal his face. Walika smiled broadly. The other girls giggled and crouched lower in the water.

"John Wes-ley," Walika called softly, melodiously, seductively. He stared and did not move.

Walika stood slowly until her body was exposed above her thighs. Her wet body sparkled in the bright sunlight. Rivulets of water ran over her full breasts and flat belly, and down her slender brown legs.

John Wesley was mesmerized. His jaw hung. He could not move.

Walika took a step toward the shore.

John Wesley bolted. The brush closed abruptly and was still. The girls giggled, then laughed loudly. They splashed each other, and one charged Walika and pushed her over, laughing wildly.

Howahkan's party rode in a sparse aspen grove. There was no discernible trail, and riders found their own paths. They moved closer and converged as they approached a cut in the mountain range. The trail narrowed when they entered the canyon. The steep walls of the canyon closed in on the riders and forced them to ride single-file on a game trail alongside a narrow stream. The tumbling stream occasionally sent up plumes of spray that wet the riders and their mounts.

The shadow of the canyon rim cast by the dying sun seemed to race up the opposite rocky face of the canyon, and the light vanished quickly. Howahkan signaled a halt in the gathering gloom.

Camp was pitched in an opening in the canyon alongside the cascading stream. Huge conifers cast dark moon shadows over the camp. A half dozen fires were built about the camp and soon provided light and heat. Some men opened packs of pemmican while others laid out bedding. Some stood at fires, turning front and back to warm themselves.

Michael and Kimimela sat on a log near a fire, chewing on chunks of pemmican. The first time he had tasted the trail food, he had found it unpalatable. He had since developed a taste for it. Michael scooped up a handful of forest detritus at his feet and rubbed his greasy hands. He turned to Kimimela.

"Tell me about the Celestials."

She looked at him, then at the fire. "They are ... a mystery to me. Howahkan deals with them alone. He says little to me."

"Where do they come from?" Michael said.

Kimimela stood. "You will see, and you will know what Howahkan wants you to know." She rubbed her hands together and warmed them at the fire.

"Kimi."

She looked at him.

"When you were correcting the Reverend's theology, you called him an American. Why?"

"Of course, he's American." She looked puzzled.

"Why not wasichu?" he said.

She looked up. "Hmm. I see. I don't know."

Howahkan's party was on the trail. On a succession of days, they rode on a canyon trail, through aspen groves in high mountains, and in an oak forest along a modest stream. The party then descended from the high country through foothills to a rolling plain. After riding a few hours, the rolling country gave way to a broad flat meadow. They rode on a faint trail alongside a dark fringe of willows and oak that only partially obscured the broad river beyond.

The trail left the river and climbed a gentle slope to a treeless ridge. At the top of the ridge, Howahkan signaled a stop. The warriors bunched up behind the leaders. Kimimela leaned over and removed Michael's blindfold. He rubbed his eyes.

Below, a broad valley lay between parallel ranges of low hills. A wide river in the middle of the valley stretched to the horizon miles away where it disappeared in a cut between the two ranges. At the base of the hill, there was a substantial pier of weathered wood planks at the river's edge. A faint trail in zigzag switchbacks ran from the hilltop where they sat their horses down the slope to the pier.

Michael was puzzled. *What was this pier doing here in the wilderness? It surely was used, but for what purpose? And by whom?*

Howahkan raised his arm and motioned forward. The party made its sinuous way down the hillside toward the pier.

The young people's meeting had ended, and girls and boys stood about, talking and moving away. Rufus sauntered away, hands in pockets. He pulled his hand from a pocket and waved over his shoulder to John Wesley.

John Wesley gathered his papers and two drawings that he had used for illustrations. He looked up to see that all had gone except Walika. Walika stood where she had sat. She and John Wesley simply stared at each other. She smiled impishly and turned away.

She hurried to catch up with Rufus. She walked beside him, looking up at him, talking animatedly, gesturing with both hands. He nodded occasionally, looked down at her, nodded, then walked on, looking at the ground as they rounded a tipi and disappeared.

John Wesley sat on a bench under the arbor. Rufus leaned against a pillar that supported the roof. Rufus was talking, and John Wesley listened. John Wesley stared at his hands on the table before him. Then he looked up at Rufus.

Rufus never stopped talking. It was a one-way conversation. At one point, Rufus left the pillar and leaned toward John Wesley. He waggled a finger in his face, then stepped back and leaned against the pillar. He looked out to the stream and the horse herd grazing beyond.

John Wesley stared at his hands.

A stooped figure moved silently in the dark village. The figure was covered with a blanket over his head and shoulders. He walked down the lane, then left the lane, passed two tipis and stopped beside another. He looked closely at the wall of the tipi. The moonlight illuminated the painted figures of a buffalo, a stick figure in front of the buffalo brandishing a spear, and a lightning bolt overhead.

John Wesley lowered the blanket from his head. He shivered. He knelt beside the tipi. The bottom of the hide wall was rolled up and held in place with two forked sticks. He placed his hand on the ground under the rolled wall. A hand from inside appeared under the rolled hide and rested on his. He lay down slowly and scooted carefully and quietly under the rolled wall.

Inside the tipi, Walika raised her cover robe, and John Wesley slowly slid under. He reached for her and ran his hand over her naked body from her shoulder to her hip. She placed his hand on her breast. He shivered from his head to his toes. She put her arms around him and held him tightly until he was still.

As she helped him remove his trousers, a muffled sound came at their feet. Walika froze and put her hand lightly on John Wesley's mouth. Walika's mother was shifting in her bed. They waited until all was quiet.

John Wesley pushed his trousers off with a foot. He pulled her to him and felt her warm body against his. He had never before felt so close to Heaven. He rolled over on top of her and kissed her hard. She shrank back at first from the unfamiliar kiss, then relaxed and kissed him back.

She pushed him gently from her and turned over. John Wesley was perplexed. *What did I do wrong?* He was not skilled at sexual affairs, but he had overheard the talk of boys who did not know his chosen profession.

Walika lifted her bottom to him and put his hand on her hip. She moved her bottom slowly side to side. John Wesley decided that she knew more about coupling than he, and he responded. Her reaction told him that he was performing as the savage technique required.

Their lovemaking was fumbling at first, then intense and finally explosive. At her climax, Walika gasped and cried softly, "Ahhh, umph!"

There was a rustling from her mother's bed. "Are you all right, daughter?" her mother said softly.

Walika held her breath. "Yes, mother," she squeaked. There was another rustling from her mother's direction as she shifted her covers. Walika exhaled slowly.

John Wesley wiped the sweat from his cheek. He withdrew from Walika and lay on his side. She turned on her side to face him. He kissed her face and her neck and caressed her breast. How could he leave?

She provided the answer. She pulled away from him and reached for his pants at the bottom of her bed. She helped him struggle into them. When he had finished, she pulled him to her and kissed him, inexpertly but passionately. Then she raised the bed cover and pushed him toward the tipi wall.

He scooted to the wall, then leaned back to kiss her once more. She touched his cheek, placed her hand over his mouth, and pushed him again lightly toward the wall. He rolled under and was gone.

# CHAPTER SIXTEEN

## The Celestials

Howahkan and Maloskah stood at the pier's edge, talking in low tones. Warriors wandered idly about the pier. The reins of mounts were tied to willows near the pier. Pack-horses and their handlers stood quietly on the grassy bench behind the pier. The horses were held closely by lead ropes. Some of the animals dropped their heads to graze.

Everyone, whatever they were doing and wherever they stood, peered downstream, squinting in the bright sunshine. Michael and Kimimela stood near the tethered mounts. Kimimela stared at the saddle where the river pierced the range.

"What are we looking for?" Michael said. She said nothing. She stared downstream, oblivious of his presence. "Kimi?"

"Wait," she said, still staring at the cleft in the mountain.

Michael stared and saw nothing. He was becoming impatient and a bit annoyed. But he waited.

"There!" Kimimela said. "Look!" She pointed toward the saddle.

Michael looked. He strained and saw nothing. His irritation increased. "Would you please tell me what the hell—"

"There! Look!" She pointed again.

He saw it. It was a faint image on the water that wasn't there when he looked before. Minutes passed, and it gradually enlarged as it moved closer. Slowly it took on the contours of a vessel.

Or was it? There were no sails, no masts. It appeared to glow a brilliant yellow in the bright sunlight. Red accents outlined prominent features of the ship. Yellow and orange pennants flew from staffs.

The ship sailed closer. No, it didn't sail, it glided, seeming to emit a humming, throbbing sound. Michael frowned. *What is this thing?*

The ship glided to the dock and gently nudged the pilings. Crew aboard the ship threw lines to warriors standing on the pier. The Indians pulled the slack from the lines, wrapped them around stanchions and tied them. When the ship was secured to the pier, the humming and throbbing declined and ended. All was quiet.

Michael looked at Kimimela. He opened his mouth to speak.

"Not now," she said.

A wide gangway sloped from the deck of the ship down to the pier. The pack animals were lined up on the pier near the gangway. The Beothuk handlers held the animals' lead ropes and watched the crew members on board scurrying about, securing lines, and moving goods on the deck.

Michael and Kimimela stood nearby. They also watched. Michael was entranced. The ship and its crew were so different, so bizarre, that he had a hard time accepting what he was seeing.

The Celestials were an Asian people. They wore loose cotton trousers and loose shirts of soft pastel colors, yellow, red, blue, maroon. Their trousers were bound up with cotton sashes. Most wore headbands of similar colors. Some wore earrings of gold.

Some of the Celestials also wore engraved and colored disks around their necks or attached to their clothing. Michael looked at Kimimela. She wore a similar disk affixed to her dress. When he had asked her about it, she had smiled but offered no explanation about its origins.

The preparation on deck appeared to be finished, and the offloading began. A line of Celestials carried bundles wrapped in colored cloth from the deck to the pack animals. The Celestials laid the bundles on the pier and walked back up the gangway for another load.

The Beothuk packers loaded the bundles into the panniers of the pack animals, adjusting and repositioning until the contents of the panniers were stable and balanced side to side.

Michael turned to Kimimela. "I can assume what these bundles contain. Do you know?"

"Of course. It is no secret to you now. Balls that explode, rifles, projectiles, ammunition, other things like that."

Michael nodded.

Howahkan stood with two Celestials at the bottom of the gangway. The Celestials wore richly brocaded robes that reached their ankles. Around their necks, they wore necklaces of gold with inlaid precious stones.

Howahkan beckoned to two warriors who stood nearby. Each held a package to his chest, obviously heavy since they labored under the weight. The warriors walked to Howahkan. He nodded to them, and they handed the bundles to the two Celestials. The men hefted the bundles, testing their weight.

One of the Celestials, who appeared to be the principal

authority, gestured to two crew members who stood near-by. The two scurried over and took the packages from the principals. The Celestial chief opened one of the packages and looked at the gold bars. He stepped over to the man who held the other bundle and opened it. Satisfied now, he smiled at Howahkan and bowed sharply. He nodded to the two who held the bundles, and they carried their loads up the gangway.

The two principals bowed again to Howahkan and walked toward the gangway. Howahkan watched them a moment, then turned and walked to the pack animals.

• • • •

Howahkan's party rode in twos and threes through an aspen forest. Warriors rode closely on each side of the line of packhorses. Panniers were full and bulging. Each of ten handlers held the lead rope of a packhorse to which was tied the lead of the packhorse behind. Michael and Kimimela rode in front of the pack animals and behind Howahkan and his companion. Michael's bandanna mask was firmly in place.

The trail left the aspen and crossed a broad meadow of green switchgrass that rolled like ocean swells in the light breeze. At the far edge of the meadow, Howahkan signaled a halt and turned off the trail. The others followed.

Camp was set up in a grove of towering ponderosa pines. Warriors sat around a half dozen campfires, talking softly and chewing wasna. Kimimela and Michael sat at a fire opposite Howahkan.

"Understand, Ambassador," said Howahkan, "both sides have the same problems. We have families that we must protect. Most of the wasichu soldiers have no fami-lies here, but when your farmers move here, your soldiers cannot protect them."

"But you counsel peace," Michael said.

"We do, but Taloka and other angry people do not, and the wasichu leaders do not understand that there are different Indians, just as there are different Americans."

"Yes," said Michael. "And sometimes the army must do what Washington commands, not what the local commander wishes."

"Ambassador, Michael, you must convince your officers and your Great White Father that The People have better weapons. You have seen them. We could destroy your forts and kill your soldiers in the forts. But we do not. We know the world has changed."

"I understand," Michael said. "May I tell the major about these armaments?"

Howahkan looked into the fire a long moment. He looked up at Michael. "You may tell him that you have seen them. You must not tell him about the Celestials. We have the advantage, and we must keep it. Not to destroy, but to preserve peace. Do you understand?"

"I understand," said Michael.

"Do you believe me when I say I want to avoid war?"

"Yes," Michael said. "I do."

"I trust you, Ambassador, Michael."

Howahkan's party rode into the outskirts of their village. Villagers saw them coming and ran toward the kiva. When the riders arrived there, the villagers greeted them and took the reins of their horses.

Kimimela reached over to Michael and removed the blindfold. He rubbed his eyes and smiled at her. "Now all is well," he said. "I see you." She smiled faintly and looked around to see who was listening. Two women standing nearby smiled and whispered to each other.

Maloskah stepped from the throng of people and greeted Howahkan. Maloskah handed Howahkan a small pouch. Howahkan hefted the pouch and handed it to Michael.

Michael took the pouch, nodded and turned toward the lane. He glanced at Kimimela as he stepped off toward his tipi. Her countenance was blank.

Michael sat on a blanket on the ground in the center of his tipi. The small desk rested on his lap. The code card lay on the desktop. A coded message was written at the top of the sheet that he held. Below the coded message, the text in plain English was written in his hand.

He read to himself: "Urgent. Tell Howahkan we need land he calls Valley of Plum Trees for settlement. Will pay. Not negotiable." Michael looked up. He frowned.

"Now it begins," he said aloud.

• • • •

Michael stood at the kiva entrance with Howahkan and Maloskah. Michael held Major Burke's message.

Howahkan scowled at Michael. "Why does he say this?" Howahkan said in an angry voice that surprised Michael. "He knows my answer! This is not good. Tell him!"

Howahkan glared at Michael, turned and strode away. Maloskah stood a moment, looking at Michael, turned and followed Howahkan.

Michael watched them go. He pondered, *This is the way wars begin. Two antagonists intent initially on having their own way agree to talk. Both sides appear willing to make concessions, eager to avoid conflict. Then one side makes a demand that both sides know is not negotiable. The result can only be conflict.*

Michael walked down the lane to his tipi, head down and reeling from the turn of events. *This must not happen.* He had too much at stake on both sides of the frontier.

He pulled back his tipi's entrance flap and went inside. He picked up his lap desk and sat down on a blanket on the ground beside the fire pit. He opened the top and took out a blank sheet of paper and the code card.

He wrote on the blank sheet: "Answer same. Not for sale. Urge no settlement. Serious consequences. Are discussion and reason no longer options?"

Michael walked to Maloskah and a warrior who stood at the hitching rail of the kiva. The warrior held the reins of his horse. Michael handed the message pouch to Maloskah who passed it to the warrior without comment. The warrior pushed the pouch into a satchel he wore on a strap across his back. He mounted quickly and kicked his horse into a gallop.

Maloskah and Michael watched him as he splashed through the stream at the ford. Michael turned to Maloskah. He wanted Maloskah to talk with him, to tell him that he understood that Michael was not responsible, that he knew that Michael had only the best interests of the Beothuk people at heart. Maloskah nodded and walked toward the kiva entrance.

Michael felt his world slipping away. He looked around. For the first time since he had arrived in the village six weeks ago, he felt insecure, a United States Army soldier in an Indian village, an ambassador, a representative of a foreign government that seemed intent on depriving The People of their land and their past.

He walked aimlessly. Nothing seemed familiar. It was if he had just arrived and saw the village with the eyes of a newcomer, an outsider. He wore all Beothuk clothing, and he felt like an imposter.

Then he saw Kimimela. She sat on a bench under the arbor. Lalowa, a middle-aged friend whose tipi lay adjacent to hers, stood behind Kimimela and plaited her hair. She had finished one braid that hung below her waist and was almost finished on the second. Four women sat in a circle on the ground, beading and talking and laughing.

He walked to the arbor. Kimimela looked up and smiled. Lalowa nodded and said nothing, not wishing to intrude. Michael leaned on a corner post and watched. And it all flowed back. Watching this quiet domestic scene, he felt once again at ease and secure. This was the woman he loved, and this was where he wanted to be.

She smiled again, but still said nothing. Michael suspected that she felt constrained by Lalowa's presence. No doubt she would have had a response to Michael's gaze had they been alone.

He noticed that the four beading women looked toward the kiva and followed their gaze. He saw a pack train of a dozen horses with bulging packs moving slowly into the village toward the kiva. Six men dressed in skin clothing led the horses. Michael suspected that they were white, though it was difficult to be sure because of their weathered skin. The heavy beards gave them away.

Kimimela noticed Michael's stare. She turned and saw the pack train. She stood, pulling on the finished second plait. "Thank you, Lalowa."

Lalowa nodded to Kimimela, then to Michael, and walked away.

Michael spoke, still watching the procession. "Who are they? What are they doing here?"

Kimimela walked over to him. "They come every year

at this time to pay the fee."

"The fee?"

"Trapping used to be dangerous for trappers. Some Indian people didn't like for them to kill the animals and take their skins away. But now the confederation brings peace, and the trappers pay ten percent of their catch in skins or coin."

Michael frowned. "This works? The trappers are okay with this?"

"Of course!" she said. "They also have accepted limits. We reduce the number of animals they can take from streams that seem to be over trapped."

"Amazing. That's . . . amazing," he said.

Kimimela smiled at his reaction. She looked again at the pack train. The trappers had reached the kiva and were tying reins to a hitching rail. Howahkan and Maloskah and two other warriors walked over to them. Howahkan greeted them, and all shook hands.

Suddenly Kimimela straightened. Her eyes opened wide. "Oh, no!"

Michael stiffened. "What?"

She pointed at the trappers. "The man who just took off his cap. I think ... I think . . . that is the man who wanted to marry me, who made the marriage offer."

She stared hard. They were about fifty yards away. "Yes . . . yes . . . I'm sure of it!" She moved closer to Michael.

Michael and Kimimela watched. As if he sensed their stare, the trapper who talked with Howahkan turned and looked in the direction of the arbor. He saw Kimimela. He turned only a fraction, and he faced her squarely, staring at her.

Kimimela leaned toward Michael. "He scares me," she

said softly, without taking her eyes from the trapper.

Michael stared at the trapper a moment, then moved slowly to stand in front of Kimimela. The trapper raised his chin slightly, as if in challenge. He turned back to Howahkan and said something. Howahkan nodded, then turned and walked toward the kiva entrance. The trapper turned back to stare at the arbor. He stood there a moment, then followed Howahkan into the kiva.

Kimimela put her arms around Michael's waist and held him close. Michael turned and pulled her beside him, encircling her shoulders with his arm. She stiffened and pulled away from him. She looked around to see whether anyone had seen. She looked up at him and smiled. For a moment, she had forgotten who she was.

"I don't usually tattle-tale," Rufus said, "but I think I got to this time." Rufus and Michael walked down the lane toward the bottom of the village. Rufus had shed his uniform piece by piece, as had Michael. Now both, strolling on a path in a Beothuk village, looked like warriors or traders.

Michael waited. Rufus seemed still to be contemplating whether or how much to tell.

"The young reverend may be makin' a peck of trouble for hisself and others as well. He's been cavortin' with a pretty little piece on the sly. He's been under the tipi wall at least once. I'm sorry to say that I helped set it up. I thought it was a kick, the Reverend's son and all that, but I had some afterthoughts. That's why I'm telling ya' now.

"I thought it would be just uh one-time thang, you know, getting a little Indian piece—uh, well, sorry, sir."

"Go on," Michael said.

"Well, it waren't no casual one-time thang. He's still making out on the sly. I saw 'em just yesterday layin' on the bank downstream, him with his hand up her dress and her kinda enjoyin' it."

Michael pondered. "I know that family. They are related somehow to Kimimela. There are two big brothers who would be after young Throckmorton if they knew about this. She's old enough for courting, but she hasn't had her coming out. Anyway, what young Throckmorton is doing could not be considered courting."

Michael stopped and turned to Rufus. "Talk with John Henry. Tell him how serious this is. He can get the girl in a whole mess of trouble. He can leave it all behind him when he goes, but she still has to live in this village. If he isn't responsive, tell me. Then I'll talk to him."

"I'll do it," Rufus said. "I'll put the fear of God and Kanta Kawan in him. I'd hate to see him face up to Throckmorton senior if he finds out about it. God Almighty! That old boy would boil him in oil and cook him on the fires of Hades!"

Michael smiled, then sobered. "It's no laughing matter, Rufus. This could escalate into a major problem."

# CHAPTER SEVENTEEN

### The Little Indian Girl Is Not Available

The village was quiet. Two women stood under the arbor, talking softly. Three children played on the ground nearby. A dog trotted up the lane past Kimimela's tipi. Not a breath of air stirred. The morning sun was warm, not yet hot. A long rack beside Kimimela's tipi was loaded with strips of meat for drying.

In front of the rack, Kimimela sat on her knees on a deerskin that was stretched and staked to the ground. She bent over the hide and scraped with a broad, sharp blade. Michael sat cross-legged on the ground near her. He wore all Indian clothing. He watched Kimimela as she methodically scraped, taking care to remove the flesh without cutting the skin. Kimimela was absorbed in her work. She occasionally grunted as she scraped. She ignored Michael.

After watching in silence, he said, "You look like an Indian."

She leaned back on her heels. She brushed a loose strand of long brown hair from her face. "Well, you noticed. Just because I'm smarter than you and speak more languages than you doesn't mean that I can't also be an Indian." She stared at him.

He tried to read her face, her peculiar look with lips pursed and eyebrows raised ever so slightly. Was it a look of pity, or defiance, or superiority, or boredom, or just plain fun?

She leaned forward on all fours and returned to her scraping. He watched her, and his face clouded. *I love this woman. Now what am I going to do about her?*

"What am I going to do about you?" he said softly. There was no humor in the question.

She sat back on her heels and looked at him. She knew well what his expression and his question meant. But she responded lightly. "Oh my, the big wasichu doesn't know what to do with the little Indian girl. Poor boy." She looked grim, annoyed. Then a smile played about her lips.

"Oh, I know what to do with the little Indian girl," he said. He leaned forward and reached for her. She jerked backward.

"You stay where you are, wasichu, or I'll call for help. There are some people here who would be glad for a reason to jump on you."

Michael smiled.

"The trapper, for one," she said. She leaned back. "Did you know that he raised his offer? A hundred horses, a hundred skins and fifty dollars coin."

"The little Indian girl is not available."

She stared at him. Her face was a mask, blank. He frowned. That look! He tried again to read her face, with no success. She bent over the hide and returned to scraping.

"Has Howahkan said anything to you about Plum Valley?" he said.

"Don't ask me. You talk to him. You haven't received anything?"

"Nothing," he said. "It's not like the major."

Suddenly, shouts were heard from the direction of the kiva. These were followed by muffled, excited voices.

Then Howahkan, Maloskah and two others walked from behind the kiva, talking and gesturing excitedly. They saw Michael and Kimimela and strode rapidly down the lane toward them.

Michael saw them coming. They were grim, jaws clenched, and he knew that this was not good. He stood.

Howahkan began to speak when they were still a dozen paces away. "They have done it!" he said with uncharacteristic heat. "Soldiers have set up a camp in Plum Valley! Farmers are there."

Michael spoke slowly, softly, more to himself than others. "That's why I received no reply."

Howahkan calmed. "Talk is finished, Ambassador," he said firmly, but sadly, it seemed. Howahkan turned and walked away. Maloskah hesitated, stepped toward Michael, as if he wanted to say something, stopped, and turned to follow Howahkan.

John Wesley and Walika sat on the stream bank in their secluded hideaway, protected by the thicket of rushes, cattails and willows.

"This latest trouble," he said, "I know that it means that we will be leaving. I don't want to go, but I must." He touched her cheek, and she put her hand over his. She had not understood his words, but she understood. A tear rolled down her cheek. He wiped it away and kissed her lips softly.

She reached for him, and they held each other tightly. She pulled back and opened the drawstring of a small skin bag in her lap. She reached into the bag and took out a little pouch. The pouch of soft deerskin was fringed and decorated with short quills, colored red and green, and tiny glass trade beads.

She handed the small pouch to John Wesley. "I do . . . for you," she said softly in English. He took the pouch and examined it, turning it over and over. His eyes glistened, and he could say nothing. She put both hands to her face to hide her tears. He pulled her to him and held her.

The Throckmortons stood with Howahkan, Michael and Kimimela outside the kiva. All were saying their goodbyes and the Reverend Throckmorton his God blesses.

About a hundred people stood about talking, whispering, watching the proceedings. Rufus was among the group, chattering and laughing. Whether the people were here to say goodbye to the holy man or to break the monotony was uncertain from their demeanor.

The Reverend Throckmorton shook the hands of Howahkan, Michael and Kimimela, thanked them for their kindnesses and wished them well. Howahkan, Michael and Kimimela withdrew, leaving the Throckmortons standing before the people.

John Wesley had not heard the conversation with Howahkan, and he had not taken part in the goodbyes. Since he and his father had arrived at the kiva a half hour ago, he had had eyes only for Walika.

She stood at the front of the group of spectators, looking at John Wesley, watching his every move. There was pain in her face, like an injured animal. They both searched for answers to unasked questions.

The Reverend John Wesley Throckmorton looked tired. He sagged like his battered black suit. His face was drawn, and the lines had deepened in the last two weeks. He turned to his son. "It has been an exhilarating and frustrating experience, John Wesley. But it has not been without reward. It is a beginning." He looked out at the people and smiled benevolently.

Then he sobered. He turned to his son. "But it is only a small beginning. Would you be willing, John, to return to this village to continue what we have begun?"

John and Walika stared into each other's eyes. "I would, Father." He turned away so his father would not see the tears welling up in his eyes. "With all my heart."

# CHAPTER EIGHTEEN

A Fragrance of Cinnamon Oil

A force of about three hundred Indians moved stealthily, hiding behind the heavy waist-high brush. Most of the body were Beothuk, but there were confederates as well, Lakota, Cheyenne, Arapaho, a delegation of visiting Utes.

The leading skirmishers parted the brush. They saw a hundred yards away a sizable army encampment set up in a flat. The flat ended at a bank that sloped sharply down to a shallow stream. Three neat lines of tents paralleled the stream. A dozen empty wagons, their shafts on the ground, were parked haphazardly behind the tents. A few soldiers wandered about, chatting idly.

Howahkan and Maloskah, crouching behind the lines of skirmishers, looked at each other, the same questions on their minds. Where were the cooking fires? The lines of drying laundry? The stacked rifles? The troopers' horses? The troopers?

Just beyond the encampment, on a slight rising, the walls of a large stockade were under construction. Two walls built of sturdy vertical logs were near completion. Workers moved about busily. The muffled sounds of the construction, the pounding of sledges, shouted orders, logs and planks being lowered and dropped into place, were carried to the Indians by the gentle breeze.

The Indians were fascinated. This was the first walled army structure the Indians had seen. Their curiosity satisfied, they moved into position. Hidden by brush, warriors loaded rounds into their repeating rifles and attached grenades to their belts. A few warriors carried the tubular shoulder weapons. They hefted them and checked them over. On whispered commands, the warriors spread right and left and formed skirmish lines. Others set up mortars and stacked projectiles on the ground beside the small cannon.

Howahkan nodded to Maloskah who returned the nod. "All right," Howahkan said. Maloskah lifted his rifle to his shoulder and aimed toward the army position. He fired twice in rapid succession.

The skirmish lines seemed to explode, as all fired together. The following rifle fire was sporadic and continuous. Mortars boomed, sending their projectiles arcing into the sky toward the army encampment. Shoulder-held weapons blasted wagons and tents.

Then Howahkan's and Maloskah's unspoken fears were confirmed. From their hiding places behind the stream embankment and large rocks scattered about the flat, hundreds of soldiers rose and returned fire.

It became quickly apparent that this was a new battle. The soldiers fired with repeating rifles. Some soldiers fired the shoulder-held tubular weapons. The thump of mortars from the soldiers' lines was followed by the whine of overhead projectiles and explosions in the Indians' lines.

Surprised warriors shrank behind their sparse cover and searched around for more substantial protection. The furious firing continued for another hour, with casualties on both sides.

Howahkan decided that the battle would not be won. He ordered a ceasefire and withdrawal. A few warriors continued to fire as others gathered the wounded and as many of their dead as they could reach without endangering themselves. That done, the Indians abandoned their positions and withdrew.

• • • •

Michael stood with Howahkan, Maloskah and two others. Howahkan glared at Michael.

"I swear. I know nothing of this," Michael said. "I told them nothing."

Howahkan simply stared, pain etched on his face. "You are finished here," he said. "You must go."

Michael stooped and emerged from his tent. He straightened. He wore his full army uniform. It felt strange, unfamiliar, new and foreign. He untied the reins of his horse from a stake and mounted. He rode slowly up the lane. People stood in front of their tipis. They watched him ride by, some with looks of hate, others bland, others curiosity.

Kimimela stood in front of her tipi. Her face was a mélange of anger, pain, love. Her eyes glistened. When he was before her tipi, he stopped. What must he do? What could he do? She turned away and entered her tipi.

He shook his reins and rode on.

Michael rode on a trace that passed as a trail on the short grass prairie. The midday sun burned the back of his neck and sucked the moisture from under his arms. He removed his hat and wiped the sweat from his forehead with his sleeve. He squinted in the glare. He replaced the hat and rode on. He slumped in the saddle and swayed with the rhythm of the horse's gait.

Night brought sweet relief from the heat. Bright moonlight dimly illuminated the grassy slope, describing shapes of large rocks and scrub juniper and pine. Michael weaved and swayed in the saddle. He was more asleep than awake.

He straightened and pulled his mount up. He looked around. He had dozed and lost the trail. He turned his mount, shook the reins and rode back up the slope until he found the faint markings of the trail. He rode down the trace, rattled by the jostling. He wondered in his sleep-deprived condition if he were descending into the jaws of hell.

Morning, and the sun already burned fiercely. Michael rode slowly into the fort and pulled up on the parade ground. A soldier walked over and took his mount's reins. The soldier sensed that the lieutenant was in no mood for military bearing and did not salute.

Michael nodded, untied his saddlebag and slid it off. He threw the bag over his shoulder and walked to his quarters. He opened the door of his room. This was one of the rooms in the small two-room plank building that he shared with another junior officer. Dropping the bag on the floor, he collapsed on the bed. He lay there, fully clothed, staring at the ceiling.

Michael sat with Major Burke on the porch of the commandant's house. He rocked slowly in his wicker rocker and sipped his iced drink.

"It's out of my hands," the major said. "Settlement will proceed. And not just in Plum Valley."

"What's happening?" Michael said. "Peace seemed possible."

"It was a peace that did not include settlement," Burke said. "Washington wouldn't have it."

They sipped their drinks and rocked. A gentle breeze on the shaded porch provided a respite of sorts from the heat.

"How did you get the weapons?" Michael said.

"Not me. My replacement."

Michael stopped rocking abruptly and turned toward the major. "Your replacement?"

Burke looked out to the parade. It was empty. The only movement was the flag that fluttered weakly in the light breeze. He turned back to Michael.

"I have disagreed with policy for a long time. That's why I sent you to The People. I thought we could do some good before the cavemen in Washington acted. When Washington turned belligerent, I decided that I would have no part of it and asked for early retirement. It came through, and my replacement is here. You'll meet him."

"The weapons?" Michael said.

"The Celestials approached us. Strangest thing you ever saw. Five Asian men, dressed in flowing colored robes, ride into the post on beautiful thoroughbred stallions, decorated, like for a parade. They rode straight for my office. Without asking anyone where to go. As if they knew.

"I was with my replacement. He had arrived only the day before. The Celestials came right in, with my orderly shouting that they couldn't do that. They spoke good English and outlined what they had to offer. They are interested in profits, Lieutenant, not ideology. They'll sell to anybody. My replacement, the youngest major in the army, mind you, was delighted. He's a dangerous man. Pity The People. And his own troops."

Michael stared at his empty glass, then raised his head to look at Burke. "How long did it take to deliver the goods?"

Burke smiled. "Oh, the Celestials knew the army would buy. They delivered the next day. They had anticipated what the army would buy, and they had it stashed and guarded a two-hour ride from the fort. How in hell they could have moved that quantity of goods without our patrols seeing them is beyond me.

"Very strange," Michael said. "Did they train the troops in the use of the weapons? I was told that they came to the Beothuk village with the first purchase and stayed a week."

"Same here. They sent ten men with the first shipment. Stayed a week. That's all we needed. Then they left. They said they would send a dispatch periodically to take our next order.

Cheeky bastards."

Michael rocked, frowning. His mind raced. "When do you leave?" he said.

"Week, two weeks, month max. Won't take long to get young Bentley checked in. He figures he already knows everything worth knowing."

Major Burke sobered and leaned toward Michael. His expression was grim. "Michael, Washington wants a decisive battle. Bentley is their man. He intends to destroy the main village of The People. He figures that will break them. And he's right. With the new armaments from the Celestials, he'll have the means to do it."

"What's to be done?" Michael said.

"That's for you to chew on," Burke said. "I don't know. Bentley is not a rational man."

Burke stood, and Michael followed. They deposited their glasses on the small round serving table between the rockers. Michael turned to leave.

"By the way," Major Burke said. Michael stopped and turned back to him. "Take care if you talk about the Point," Burke said. "He was at the bottom of his class."

A cadre of the fort's officers sat on three sides of the rectangular table. Major Burke was there, and Captain Jackson and Lieutenants Worth and Wagner.

On the fourth side sat Major Fredrick Scott Bentley. Short, lean and muscular, Bentley's carelessly trimmed ample mustache, which drooped down on each side of his thin lips, was not sufficient to hide a plain, ruddy face. Full blond curls that any young girl would envy reached his shoulders. Michael wrinkled his nose. He was sure he smelled a hint of a fragrance of cinnamon oil. His pondering was broken by Major Bentley's voice.

"I am pleased with the fort at Plum Valley," Bentley said, smiling. "Well done. The posting there has thinned our ranks a bit, but the reinforcements will arrive within days. I intend to make this post the most effective on the frontier. We want results, gentlemen, and we shall have them." He looked around the table and smiled.

"Dismissed," Bentley said.

Everyone stood. The subordinates saluted, and Bentley returned the salute. They turned to leave.

"Lieutenant Wagner," Bentley said. "Stay, please."

Michael turned back and stood before the table. The others went through the door, and the door closed.

"Sit, please," Bentley said. The lieutenant and the major sat down.

Bentley studied Michael, frowning, tensed, his eyes locked on Michael's. This is bizarre, Michael thought to himself. Did he study theater? Was he an actor?

Bentley relaxed, leaned back, turned aside in his chair

and crossed his legs. "Major Burke has briefed me on your mission to The People. Interesting."

"Thank you, sir," Michael said.

"I want you to return to the village."

Michael straightened. Then he sagged. "I won't be welcome, sir."

Bentley smiled. He leaned back in his chair. "Yes, I understand they were a bit surprised at Plum Valley. I was there, you know."

Michael looked blankly. Bentley noticed.

"All right, I understand that you became close to The People, and that may be useful. I want you to go back, convince them that you wish to renew your mission. Talk of peace. You will study the layout of the village, the surrounding terrain, the activities of the people there and their confederates."

Bentley paused, then leaned in, as if to emphasize his point. Or to reassure Michael. "This is for ongoing intelligence, you understand. I'm sure they have done the same reconnoitering of this post." He leaned back in his chair and spoke solemnly. "You are to leave tomorrow, and report back here in ten days. Understood? Questions?"

"I understand, sir," Michael said.

Major Bentley bent over a stack of papers on the table. Michael stood and saluted. Bentley waved him off, and Michael turned and walked to the door.

Outside, Michael stood on the porch, looking up at the heavens. *Oh Lord, if you are up there and have anything to do with the ways of men, why do you permit buffoons to decide who shall live and who shall die?*

Lieutenant Wagner and Major Burke stood on the parade. Michael held the reins of his mount. They both looked up at the flag, whipping in the stiff breeze.

"I have good news," Burke said. "For me. I leave in two days. Young Bentley is anxious to see my back. Fine with me."

Michael adjusted the bag behind his saddle. He checked the girth.

"I trust you understand what this is about," Burke said.

Michael looked up. "Yes, sir."

"What are you going to do?"

"I'm not sure," Michael said.

"Lieutenant, he has set the date for the attack," Burke said. "June twenty-seventh. Ten days out. The reinforcements will be here before then."

Michael nodded. He swung into the saddle and kicked the horse into a lope.

• • • •

Michael's head throbbed until he felt that it would shatter. He rode on a shaded trail through aspen groves, and he wondered whether he would be killed before reaching the village.

He rode on a plains trail, and he wondered whether Howahkan would permit him to enter the village.

He rode on a canyon trail, and he wondered whether Kimimela would smile when she saw him, or had she chosen to forget him?

As darkness fell, the canyon walls seemed to close in on him, and he was afraid.

Michael and Kimimela stood on the banks of the stream, where they had stood many times before. He wore his Indian clothing. They watched the stream, running high after a recent hard rain. He glanced furtively at her, trying to read her face, still uncertain of his reception. He wanted to touch her, to hold her, but he could not. Not yet.

She would not look at him. She stared at the ponies across the stream, at the kingfisher sitting on the snag at the water's edge, at the sky.

"I was afraid I had lost you," he said. "I thought you would forget me."

Kimimela turned and looked at him, and her reserve melted. She smiled a sweet smile. She spoke softly. "I could not forget you." He reached for her and pulled her to him. She wrapped her arms around his waist. He squeezed her hard.

"Hey, wasichu, not so tight!" she said.

He released her. He leaned back and smiled. *What can I say to this girl? Can I ever leave her again?* He held her cheeks in both hands and kissed her lips softly.

He sat down on the ground and pulled her down beside him. He looked into her eyes and wanted to shut out everything that intruded on this peace that he felt when he was with her.

But he knew he must deal with his other reason for returning. "Kimi, the Celestials are not friends of The People. They just wish to make money. They understand frontier warfare. They will sell to anyone. They approached the army to offer the weapons. Do you believe me? Will you tell Howahkan what happened? Will you help me?"

She pondered, looked at the stream flowing deep and swift along the reedy banks. She looked up at him. "I will tell him. He may not believe you. You are not Ambassador now. You are a wasichu. You are a soldier."

"I love you, Kimi. I swear that I will never do anything that would hurt you. Or the People."

She reached up and pulled him to her. Their arms entwined, and they kissed. He buried his face in her hair, inhaling her perfume. He pulled back, his face grim. She looked up at him and frowned.

"What?" she said.

"Kimi. There is more. This new commander, Bentley, is planning a decisive battle. He intends to attack this village. He intends to destroy it. He has set a date."

She frowned. "What are we to do?"

Michael pondered. He stared at the stream without seeing it. He looked up at the sky and watched the clouds boil and flow along the horizon. He turned back to her. "Tell Howahkan everything I have told you. He will prepare the people to defend the village. Both sides will be ready. But you and I will prevent the battle."

# CHAPTER NINETEEN

## Close Your Mission

The People prepared the village for war. Earthen barriers were erected around the outer perimeters. Rows of spring-mounted metal spears were installed at places where the army was most likely to attack.

Warriors entered the village, armed with rifles, spears and bows and arrows. Their dress identified them as more than Beothuk. There were also Cheyenne, Crow, Lakota, Arapaho, Ute, Blackfoot and others. Traditional enemies now united as members of the confederation to take part in the battle that all believed could determine how they would live.

Mortars and small cannons were placed in defensive positions. Projectiles were stacked alongside. Grenades were arranged in little pyramids along defensive lines. Warriors cleaned their rifles and restrung bows. Shoulder-held weapons were cleaned and their sights adjusted.

Howahkan and Maloskah wandered among the fortifications and nodded in greeting to warriors.

The sun was directly overhead. Heat waves blurred the view of the distant hills on each side of the valley. The knee-high dry grass hung limply in the still air. Stems of scarlet and purple penstemon, now almost bare of blossoms, rose a foot above the tops of the grasses.

Michael and Kimimela sat their horses quietly, scanning the meadow for movement. Michael wiped his face with his bandanna. He wriggled against the uncomfortable, stifling wool uniform. He scratched and pulled at the sleeves and jacket. He longed for his Beothuk shirt and breechclout and leggings.

They looked across the rolling plain toward a saddle in a low ridge where a faint outline of a trail showed on the slope.

"They are late. Will they come?" Kimimela said.

"They will come," Michael said. "If what I hear of Bentley is accurate, he will make us wait."

Michael's horse whinnied and pranced. Michael held him in check. A troop of thirty or forty horsemen appeared at the top of the ridge. Two riders separated from the force and rode down the trail on the near slope. Reaching the flat, they kicked their horses into a lope. Michael shook his reins and advanced a few steps.

Major Bentley and Captain Jackson pulled up before the lieutenant. Michael saluted, and Bentley returned the salute. Jackson nodded almost imperceptibly to Michael. He cut his eyes briefly toward Bentley.

"Thank you for coming, sir," Michael said.

"Damned inconvenient," Bentley said. He looked at Kimimela. "Who is this?"

"The place was a condition of Howahkan. This is Kimimela. She will speak for Howahkan."

"I didn't bring an interpreter," Bentley said. "I don't suppose you speak Beothuk."

"Actually, I do," said Michael.

"So do I, Major," Kimimela said. "We can talk in either Beothuk or Lakota or English. Or Spanish. Or Cheyenne. Your choice."

Bentley jerked his head to the side. He was not amused. "Well, what have we got?"

"Major Bentley," Michael said. "Howahkan knows of your plan to attack the village."

"Does he now? I wonder how he learned that?"

"Howahkan asked us to tell you that The People are prepared to defend the village. They have built fortifications, and they have stockpiled armaments from the Celestials. Many warriors from the confederated tribes have come to their aid. Howahkan does not seek this battle."

"Nor do I," Bentley said. "Lieutenant Wagner, I'm afraid your informant is confused. Major Burke, is it? Major Burke is not a happy man. He has been passed over for advancement repeatedly, and now he has been retired for incompetence."

Michael frowned.

"He didn't tell you this? He wouldn't, would he? No, I do not seek battle. I seek to defend my post, just as Howahkan seeks to defend his village."

Kimimela glanced at Michael. They were unsure how to proceed.

"Are we done here?" Bentley said.

"Yes, sir," Michael said. "I will tell Howahkan what you have said."

Major Bentley and Captain Jackson turned to leave. Michael reined his horse to leave. Kimimela did not move.

"Major," Kimimela said. All stopped and pulled their horses around to face Kimimela. "Does your desire for peace include all wasichus withdrawing from Plum Valley?"

Bentley stiffened. "I find the term offensive." Kimimela

did not flinch. She simply stared at him.

"No, we will not withdraw from what you call Plum Valley. That is United States territory. We offered to pay, and it was refused."

"Soldiers have been seen in Antelope valley and in the plain around Cattail Spring," she said.

"I don't know those names, but it doesn't matter. Troopers may ride where they wish on a pleasant sunny morning," Bentley said.

Kimimela glared at Bentley. "Shall I kill him?" she said in Beothuk, without taking her eyes off Bentley.

Michael turned to her. "That would not be wise," he responded in Beothuk.

Bentley reddened. "Goddammit, Wagner, that will do!"

Kimimela whipped her horse around and galloped away. Bentley watched her a moment, seething. He calmed, then turned back to Michael. "Lieutenant Wagner, you are to close your mission at once and report to me on your return to the post."

"Yes, sir." Michael saluted. Bentley looked coolly at Michael. He did not return the salute. Michael pulled his horse around and galloped after Kimimela.

Major Bentley smiled.

Michael, Kimimela, Howahkan, Maloskah and three others sat on the ground in a circle around the cold fire pit at the center of the kiva. Michael wore his Beothuk clothing.

"I don't trust him," Kimimela said. "He has the eyes of a snake."

Howahkan stared at the ashes. He looked up at Michael. "Ambassador?"

Now it was Michael's turn to stare into the fire pit. It was the first time Howahkan had spoken directly to him since his return to the village. Michael looked up to see Howahkan looking directly at him. Howahkan nodded.

After a moment, Michael found his voice. "He has asked for more troops. They will arrive within a week. He has set a date for the attack. June twenty-seventh."

Michael paused, looked around the circle. No one spoke. They waited.

"Howahkan. Both The People and the army are strong," Michael said. "But understand. Major Bentley is irrational and puffed up. He thinks this victory will make him a great man. I think he will attack."

Howahkan nodded. "June twenty-seventh by your counting. Seven days. I will send riders to other villages and other tribes. We will be ready."

A sliver of moonlight from the open flap of Michael's tipi dimly illuminated the interior. Michael and Kimimela lay on blankets on the ground. They were naked, partially covered by a blanket. Michael rested on an elbow, looking down at Kimimela who lay on her back.

"You should be a warrior," Michael said. "You could kill your enemies with your eyes and your tongue."

"Then he would be dead."

Michael leaned over and kissed her lightly on her lips. "After you left, he ordered me to the post," he said. "Permanently."

She rolled toward him and leaned her head against his chest. "What will happen?"

He lay back on the blanket and stared at the peak. "Court martial, likely."

She moved up to rest her head in the crook of his arm. He put his arms around her and held her close.

Michael stood before his tipi. His packed saddlebags lay at his feet. He turned to look at the morning sun, a thin crescent on the horizon. He brushed his uniform tunic with both hands. He looked down at the uniform. *What games we play in our pretty suits.*

He straightened. He looked up the lane at the line of tipis where women talked and worked. He saw the kiva where three warriors stood beside their horses at the hitching rail, talking, laughing lightly. He looked at the stream bank where he had sat so many times with Kimimela. He saw the horses in the meadow across the stream, grazing on the lush grasses.

Then he saw Kimimela. She stood before her tipi up the lane. She looked directly at him. Michael stared at her. He waited. He looked at the treetops, searching for . . . what? His soul? He turned, bent and entered his tipi.

Kimimela watched Michael's tipi. She listened to birdsong from the trees that bordered the stream. She heard children's shouts and laughter as they played at the arbor.

Then Michael emerged, bending, from his tipi. He wore his Beothuk clothing. He picked up the loaded saddlebags and tossed them inside the tipi.

He looked at Kimimela who still stood in front of her tipi. She stared at him. She stood a moment longer. Then she ran to him and fell into his arms. The people all around, at their tipis or walking on the lane, stopped what they were doing to watch and smile.

Michael and Kimimela walked in the lane toward the kiva. They leaned in close, heads almost touching, speaking softly.

Olaktay walked in the lane in the opposite direction toward them. He glared at them, his face contorted in anger.

When he was abreast of them, Olaktay stepped in front of Michael, barring his way. Michael stopped, surprised.

"No!" said Olaktay. He grabbed Kimimela's arm and pulled her roughly behind him.

Michael took a step toward Olaktay. Half a dozen women and two warriors who stood nearby walked over slowly. Others within earshot walked in their direction. It was a confrontation that many had anticipated for a long time.

"You are not welcome here, wasichu," said Olaktay. "You contaminate this village. You are carrion!"

"I counsel peace, Olaktay. What do you counsel?"

"The way of the Beothuk. Pride. To live as we have always lived!"

"Time passes. For your people and for mine. We must find a way to live in peace."

"It is not peace when the wasichu lives in my country! In my village! Go away!"

Olaktay shoved Michael. The move was sudden, and Michael almost fell. He recovered his balance and advanced on Olaktay. He hoped that Olaktay bluffed.

But he had not. He charged Michael, and his shoulder plowed into Michael's chest. Both fell and hit the ground hard. They rolled on the ground and wrestled. They staggered upright, recovered and threw punches, mostly swinging wildly and finding only air.

Olaktay charged Michael again. Michael stepped aside and punched him hard on his back as he slid past him. Olaktay fell, but rolled away and sprang to his feet. Olaktay braced himself, feet spread. Never taking his eyes from Michael, he fumbled at his belt and drew a knife from a sheath at his waist.

Olaktay advanced on him, his knife extended in front of

him. Michael stepped back and looked around, searching for something, assistance or escape. He jumped backward when something flashed before him. He looked down to see the knife stick in the ground at his feet. He bent and snatched the knife from the ground, extending it before him. He glanced quickly to his side and saw Maloskah looking directly at him.

Michael had no experience in knife fighting, but a rush of adrenaline substituted for skill. The two antagonists thrust, feinted and slashed. Michael and Olaktay were soon gasping as they crouched, advanced and circled for position. Both were soon badly cut and bleeding from multiple wounds.

"Enough!"

Michael and Olaktay looked sharply aside to see Howahkan striding toward them. They lowered their knives.

"It is finished," Howahkan said.

Howahkan extended both of his hands toward the fighters. Michael grasped his knife by the blade and offered it to Howahkan, handle first. Olaktay paused, his knife still pointing at Michael, then threw his knife to the ground at Howahkan's feet.

Howahkan spoke calmly to Olaktay. "You have shamed yourself, your family and The People. Leave this village, and do not return."

Olaktay glared at Howahkan, then Michael. He turned and strode up the lane, his shoulders thrown back and his chin uplifted.

Kimimela hurried to Michael's side. Howahkan and Maloskah walked away together. The onlookers drifted away, chatting softly. Some turned to look at Michael and Kimimela.

Kimimela looked Michael up and down. His skin shirt was in shreds. Blood from many cuts stained his shirt. She smiled. "You are a mess," she said. "Do you think you are a warrior now?"

"I'll be whatever you want me to be, Kimi." He leaned toward her, but she backed away and looked around.

He smiled. He remembered again the Beothuk taboo on public display of affection. This was hard on him since he always wanted to squeeze Kimimela any time he saw her. In close proximity, the need to touch her was almost irresistible.

"What will he do?" he said.

"He will go to Taloka. He was his spy."

Howahkan, Maloskah, Michael and Kimimela sat around a warming fire in a pit near the arbor. They watched the sun set over the distant range west of the village. Lacy horizontal cloud layers were tinted pink, orange, red.

Howahkan looked into the fire. He spoke without looking up. "Twenty warriors left in the last seven days," he said, "and ten today. They will go to Taloka. He says his medicine will protect them in battle. The wasichu bullets will not harm them."

Michael looked at Howahkan. "He will join you in this fight?" Michael said.

"Yes. But I will not turn my back to him. In his vision, Taloka is the leader of The People, not Howahkan."

"Shall we kill him?" Maloskah said.

Howahkan sighed. "No, Maloskah, it is not our way. Not now."

Maloskah watched the dancing flames. He nodded.

Michael and Kimimela sat on a thick buffalo robe before a small fire in his tipi. A thin column of gray smoke rose toward the peak until it disappeared in the darkness.

"Tell me about the Beothuk today," Michael said. I know about the divisions of the Beothuk people, but they are so spread out, how do they communicate? Do they ever come together?"

"Yes, leaders of the six council fires, the divisions of the Beothuk people, meet every year in what you call summer for a council. They meet old friends, and they decide on things of importance to all the people. This is a yearly renewal of national unity. It is also a celebration. This is where they do the Heavens Dance. The Heavens Dance is the most important spiritual expression for us. Do you understand?"

"Yes," he said.

"At this gathering, the Grand Council meets. These are the four great leaders of the nation. They are selected by the headmen of the six divisions. They set policy for the Beothuk nation and approve or disapprove actions taken by the leaders of the six divisions during the past year."

"Does that work? Do they really overturn actions taken by local headmen?" Michael said.

"Not usually. I think they express an opinion that is supposed to influence the headmen. But it is the local headmen who have the power."

"I can't imagine anyone countering an action by Howahkan," he said.

"I think that too."

"What is Howahkan's position in this?" he said.

"Howahkan is one of the four leaders in the Grand Council. I think he is the most powerful. The other members and headmen everywhere ask for his advice.

His is the strongest voice in building relationships with the Americans in the new world. He also is influential because it is our band that controls Gold Hill and dealing with the Celestials."

"Do the other three leaders agree with Howahkan's vision of a new world and the necessity of working with the Americans?"

"That is a problem. They agree that the world is changing, but they do not believe as strongly as Howahkan that we should agree to anything that requires the Beothuk to change our way of life. Michael, this is not only about whether to accept a new way of living. It's about having to change belief.

"In the island times, we believed that the white men, the Strangers, belonged to the bad spirit, and if we talked with them and made peace with them, we would not go to the happy island after we died. We brought these beliefs with us to the plains. Many people today still hold to the old ways. Can you see why it is so hard for the old people to follow Howahkan when he says that we should talk with the Americans and make peace with them? It goes against our old beliefs. Howahkan was brought up in the old ways. Can you see how hard it is for him?"

The fire had burned down to glowing coals. Kimimela picked up a small piece of wood and placed it on the embers. They watched the wood glow, smoke and catch fire. Michael added a small bough to the fire. The dry wood glowed and smoked and burst into flame.

"Yes. I understand how it can be hard to do something that is contrary to long-held belief," he said. "In that sense, it may be easier for tribes to talk with each other about changes and leave the Americans out of the discussion. Like Howahkan's attempt to persuade the tribes to end raiding and war."

"Yes," she said, "but the Americans want to be part of that discussion. They want to go further. They want us to agree to boundaries between tribes. They believe that this would be the best way to end warfare and raiding among the tribes. Howahkan has not spoken out about boundaries, but he has said that a lifestyle that includes raiding has passed. Yet he worries with others about how the young men can prove their bravery without raiding and war.

"On other things, he is more convinced. Last year, Howahkan told the headmen at the summer council that we should change practices that don't make sense. He made an example of our burial practices. Things can become scarce, and it no longer makes sense to bury a man's possessions with him and to kill his best horse. And he said that the practice of parents who have lost a child giving away everything they own, even their tipi and the clothes they are wearing, no longer makes sense.

"Many headmen and members of the Grand Council believe that Howahkan goes too far. They say they agree that change is coming, but they refuse to agree to anything that includes changing the way they live. Some say that the only contact the Beothuk should have with the Americans is with the traders. They like the mirrors and cooking pots, the glass beads and wool blankets and other things that we have become accustomed to. Some say that even that contact is not good for The People. In addition to the things The People want, the traders also bring sickness and whiskey."

Kimimela and Michael fell silent and watched the flickering flames and the dancing shadows on the walls of the tipi.

She looked at him. "What else?" she said.

"Tell me about winter counts."

She stared into the fire, pondered, calling up memories. "Winter counts. That's a way of recording our history. That and stories that old men tell most days after dark around the fire. In the island times, we relied on stories that were passed from generation to generation, but that was not really reliable. We learned from the Lakota how to record what happened on hides.

"Winter counts are history and calendar. It's a record kept by a headman or an important person. The Americans name each year with a number. We name the year by something important that happened that year. These names are painted in a circle on deerskin, from the center outward.

"The year your Captain Lewis came in my great-grandfather's time was named 'Good White Man Came' by the council because he was friendly and brought gifts. My great-grandfather did not agree to that name. He didn't like Captain Lewis.

"Another year was named 'Little Coyote's Tipi Blew Away.' Another was named 'Smallpox.' Many people died that year. A year called 'Fighting in the River' was named after a battle between the Beothuk and the Crow in a river."

Michael studied her face as she spoke. When he did not respond, she frowned. He smiled. "What will this year be called?"

"It's too early. We don't know what important things will happen this year. Maybe we'll call it 'Ambassador Came.' "

"No. It will be called 'Michael Found Kimimela.' '

She smiled. "I don't think so. That's not important to The People."

"Not to you?" he said.

"Maybe to me." She looked at her hands in her lap.

"Well, it's important to me!" He grabbed her and pushed her to the ground, tickling her with both hands. She giggled, wriggled, laughed, pushed him away, but he held her tightly and tickled her all over, under her arms, her neck, her legs and her feet. She fought him and tried to tickle him. Between spasms of laughter, she tried to shush him and stifle her own laughter.

They were exhausted. He lay across her chest, and both gasped and breathed heavily. He rose on his elbows and looked at her. The firelight bathed her face in a golden glow. Her disheveled hair flew in all directions, and beads of sweat rolled down her temples. He looked into the deep pools that were her eyes and lost himself.

He sighed. "Why must it be so complicated? How do I deal with this?"

Her eyes sparkled. "What do you mean?" she said.

He kissed her lightly on her lips and slid off her. He lay beside her, raised on an elbow with a hand holding his head. His other hand caressed her breast through her dress.

"Tell me a story," he said.

"A Beothuk story?" she said, smiling.

"A Beothuk love story."

She looked up into the darkness at the peak of the tipi. "A Beothuk love story. Hmm." She pondered, searching, remembering.

She began. "There was a boy named Little Wolf who was in love with a girl named Sweet Medicine. She was so pretty that he was almost sick from looking at her and thinking about her. He had never told her of his love. He had hardly spoken to her. He was shy, and he knew that her parents watched her carefully. When they suspected that Little Wolf was interested in Sweet Medicine, her parents built a low wooden frame bed and tied her in the bed every night with rawhide strips so she could not be stolen. They also were afraid that she might want to be stolen.

"One day when Sweet Medicine was going to the stream for water, Little Wolf caught her alone. She was shy too, but he learned that she cared for him. This almost drove him crazy. He finally had the courage to talk with her father. He offered two horses for her, all the horses he owned. The father said to go away and stop talking nonsense. Little Wolf felt like he had been struck hard in the face.

"Little Wolfs friend, Rides Slow, said he would lend two horses to Little Wolf. So Little Wolf went to Sweet Medicine's father and offered four horses. Sweet Medicine's father said to go away and stop talking nonsense. Little Wolf felt like dying.

"One day when Sweet Medicine was gathering firewood, Little Wolf stepped from behind a tree to talk with her. He told her that he would die if he could not have her. He asked her to run away with him. She said that she really liked him, but she could not go against her father's wishes. She would have to be bought in the usual Beothuk way. Little Wolf felt that he could not breathe.

"Little Wolf told Rides Slow what had happened. He told him that he was so sick with love that he would do anything to win her. Rides Slow said that he would help him steal her. Anyway, Rides Slow said, she probably wants to be stolen. So they worked out a plan. Little Wolf would go inside the tipi, and Rides Slow would pull up the tipi stakes beside her bed so Little Wolf could drag her under the tipi wall. If they had to gag her, Rides Slow would help.

"In the middle of the night, Little Wolf crawled under the tipi wall. Once inside, he crept to her bed, took his knife from his belt and quietly began cutting the rawhide thongs that held Sweet Medicine. She woke up, recognized Little Wolf, and touched his leg with her hand. He shivered. Then she touched him down there through his breechclout. He jumped and cried out. Sweet Medicine's father shouted, and her mother screeched, and Little Wolf escaped through the tipi flap and ran and ran. It was morning before he returned to the village."

"Down there?" Michael said.

"Down there. Be quiet. It's my story. Little Wolf told Rides Slow what happened. He said that he was going to die since he could not have Sweet Medicine. Rides Slow said he had another plan.

"That night, Rides Slow told Little Wolf to take off all of his clothes. Rides Slow painted his naked body white all over. Then he painted vertical black stripes all over his body and black rings around his eyes. Rides Slow said that if anyone saw him tonight, they would think he was a bad spirit and would be afraid to chase him. Little Wolf said he would do anything to win Sweet Medicine, so he said he would do it.

"After dark, Little Wolf crawled under the tipi wall and began cutting the rawhide thongs that bound Sweet Medicine to the bed. She stirred and realized that it was Little Wolf again. She touched his leg. He didn't jump this time. She reached over and grasped him down there and squeezed. He jumped and cried out. The father shouted, and the mother screamed, and they jumped out of their beds.

"Little Wolf stumbled through the tipi flap and ran outside. Villagers had heard the noises and ran from their tipis, carrying rifles and spears and clubs. In the bright moonlight, they saw this strange black-and-white creature running through the village. Some wanted to shoot it, but others said that it might be a sacred being, and trouble might come to the village if they harmed it.

"Rides Slow helped Little Wolf wash the paint off his body and gave him some clothes. Little Wolf said that his life was over, and he didn't care whether he lived or died. He said he was going to go away and live a life of raiding. Maybe he would be killed, and he would no longer be in pain. Rides Slow said he would go with him.

"Little Wolf and Rides Slow traveled many days and came upon a Crow horse hunting camp. They crept up on the herd, killed the guard and stole the horses. They drove the herd to their village right up to the tipi of Sweet Medicine. Her father stood in front of the tipi. Little Wolf asked him if a hundred horses would buy Sweet Medicine. The father said that they would, but what he really had wanted all along was a son-in-law that had proven to be a strong warrior. So everybody was happy."

"A good story," Michael said. "I like Little Wolf and Sweet Medicine. I hope they were happy and had ten healthy children."

She smiled. She pushed the blanket off her and sat up. "I must go," she said.

"Yes. Soon." He pulled her back down beside him and grasped the bottom of her dress. As he pulled the dress up slowly, she reached up and took his face in her hands. She kissed him hard as he struggled with her dress.

# CHAPTER TWENTY

## We Can Paint Your Tipi

Michael bent from the waist and stepped from his tipi. He stood, stretched and pulled his Indian shirt side to side, loosening it to ease it where it was binding. He looked around. The sun was an orange glow at the eastern horizon, coloring the filmy cloud layers in soft pastel shades. Women were building fires and cleaning the ground around tipis. Children poked heads through tipi entrances, hair tousled and blinking sleepily.

Michael strolled up the lane to Kimimela's tipi. He stooped and looked inside through the entrance. She was not there. Her rumpled blankets and skins lay near the fire pit. He backed out and looked around. He saw Lalowa who occupied the adjacent tipi with her husband and two children.

"Lalowa, have you seen Kimimela?" Michael said.

"No, not since yesterday."

"Mmm. Thank you," he said.

Michael pondered a moment and turned to go.

"I heard her last night. From her tipi," Lalowa said. Michael stopped. He turned back. Lalowa grinned.

"What did you hear?" he said.

"A sort of cry, short . . . you know." She giggled. "I thought she was with you."

Michael ran to the tipi. He bent and entered through the flap. He looked around as his eyes adjusted to the dark interior. He had only seen the rumpled blankets before. Now he saw evidence of a struggle. Some blankets were thrown against the tipi wall. Contents of a small bag were scattered about the floor. He hurried to the tipi entrance, stooped and stepped out. He looked up and down the lane. He ran to two warriors who walked toward him.

"Where is Maloskah?" One of the men pointed toward the kiva. Michael bolted. Before he reached the kiva, Maloskah, Howahkan and three others walked from the kiva entrance. Michael ran to them.

"Kimimela is not here!" he gasped. "I think she has been taken!"

"How do you know this?" Howahkan said.

"You must know that she comes to me at night. She left my tipi about midnight. No one has seen her this morning."

Maloskah, Howahkan and Michael went to Kimimela's tipi. Maloskah and Howahkan stooped and looked inside. Maloskah backed out. He straightened and saw Kohana, a young warrior walking on the lane.

"Kohana, horses, quickly!" Maloskah said. He pointed to Michael and himself.

Kohana ran to the ford and splashed through the shallow stream toward the horses that were picketed near the bank.

Maloskah and Michael urged their horses at a gallop up a hillside of lush green grass and scattered bur oaks. A covey of pintail grouse exploded from the grass in front of the horses, flying in all directions.

They slowed to a walk. Michael rode a few paces behind Maloskah who leaned over one side of his horse, then the other side, following the tracks and crushed grasses on the wet slope.

They topped the hill and slowed. Maloskah pulled up, and Michael followed. Maloskah threw a leg over his horse's neck and slid off. Michael dismounted.

Maloskah squatted and studied the ground. The soil was drier here with only sparse grass. But the horse tracks were clearly outlined in the porous soil. He held up four fingers. Four horses. Maloskah pointed at the imprint of a small wedge at the edge of a hoof print. Michael squatted for a close look.

"Taloka. I cut this," Maloskah said. They mounted and rode up the trail at a gallop.

The broad meadow was bathed in the hot sun of late afternoon. Maloskah and Michael stood in the shade of a cottonwood at the edge of a small spring. A flow of no more than a finger's thickness issued from a grassy fissure in a bank. Michael wiped his mouth as Maloskah leaned over to drink from the stream. Their horses dipped muzzles into the small pool at the base of the flow.

Maloskah straightened. Water dripped from his chin as he stared into the pool. "Taloka shames The People. He shames me."

"You don't believe his vision?" Michael said.

"He has been claiming visions since he was a small boy. No one paid attention to him, except small boys."

"It was just play then?" said Michael.

"Until one small boy believed that his vision would protect him from arrows. Taloka killed that little boy . . . my brother."

Maloskah jerked the reins of his horse. The startled

animal, water dripping from its muzzle, shied and bumped Michael's horse. Michael tightened his grip on his reins and settled the frightened horse.

Maloskah grabbed a fistful of mane and swung up on his horse. He kicked the horse in the flanks and charged off at a gallop. Michael mounted quickly and rode after him.

Michael and Maloskah tied their reins to a horizontal pine branch that had almost unhorsed Michael when his mount had walked under it in the darkness.

They crept down the slope, sliding and stumbling over downed deadwood and forest litter and small loose stones. They crouched behind a large boulder. Peering around the side of the boulder, they saw it. The small campfire about a hundred yards below that had been but a prick of light when they had first seen it.

The fire threw dancing shadows on a rock wall that backed up one side of the site and the lower branches of the lodgepole pines that seemed to grow only as tall as they were illuminated. The glow of the fire also traced the outline of two men. One crouched, tending something at the fire. The other stood across the fire, watching.

Michael pulled back behind the boulder and checked his pistol. Even at this tense moment, he could not suppress a smile at his good fortune in acquiring a new six-shot pistol from the Celestials to replace his single-shot percussion pistol. The .54-caliber smoothbore was the latest army issue. The Celestial model rendered it obsolete.

Maloskah adjusted the Celestial pistol under his belt. Then he slowly drew a knife from a scabbard at his waist. He touched Michael's arm and motioned with his hand for him to move left from the boulder and up the hill behind the camp. He pointed to himself and then pointed down the hill. Michael nodded.

Maloskah crouched and crept away from the boulder, down a gradual slope, hiding behind boulders and bushes. He was quickly swallowed by the darkness.

Michael moved away from the boulder up the dark hillside. He stumbled over stones and collided with bushes and low tree branches. He stopped often, motionless and listening. When the men at the fire showed no alarm, he moved higher, sliding on the bed of needles and decayed bark.

He walked into a low-hanging stout branch, slid on the forest detritus and fell hard on his back. There was a furious thrashing and flapping of wings as a large bird took flight from the tree. He lay still and quiet where he had fallen, holding his breath. Hearing nothing, he stood slowly and looked down toward where the fire should be, but he was above the rock face that hid the fire.

He moved again, mostly on the level, then edged gradually down the slope toward the fire. He cleared the rock face behind the camp and saw the fire again. The two Indians stood on opposite sides of the fire. They had not heard the thrashing above. Or, if they heard it, they had not been alarmed.

One of the men dropped a short length of wood on the embers. Sparks flew, and the men stepped away from the fire. The dry wood ignited immediately, and the flames rose. The same warrior reached behind him for another piece of wood. The other stretched and walked away from the fire toward the darkness. He vanished into the brush beyond the circle of light. The warrior at the fire dropped the limb on the embers and watched the flames as the dry wood ignited.

Michael raised his pistol and leveled on him.

A sharp cry, followed by a muffled groan, came from

the darkness where the warrior had entered the brush. The Indian at the fire jerked a pistol from his belt. He looked around frantically.

Michael fired, and the man fell heavily into the fire, scattering sparks and embers. Echoes from the shot bounced about the canyon walls. The echoes died, and it was still. The only sound was the light breeze in the pine branches. Michael crept down the slope toward the fire. He moved from cover to cover, behind boulders and trees, his pistol at the ready.

He whirled around and pointed his pistol when he thought he heard a crunching sound on his left, but he saw nothing. He took another step toward the fire, then reeled when he was struck a hard glancing blow to the side of his head. The darkness had saved his life, but he was momentarily stunned. He lost the pistol and fell to the ground on his back.

The attacker bent over him and slashed wildly in the darkness. Michael groaned as the blade sliced across his chest. He rolled on his side and scrambled to his feet, his head swirling. He stood with feet spread and shook his head. He felt for the knife in the sheath at his belt. He found it and withdrew it.

In the moon glow, Michael saw the warrior crouched before him. The warrior held his knife in front of him, pointed at Michael's belly.

The figure spoke slowly in Beothuk. " 'Ambassador,' they call you. I am Taloka. I call you 'wasichu devil.' "

Taloka lunged and jabbed the knife at Michael. Michael jumped aside, but Taloka's blade ripped his sleeve and slashed his left arm. Michael winced and felt the warm blood run down his arm.

Michael countered with a knife thrust at Taloka's head.

Taloka jerked backward, and the knife sliced Taloka's ear. He thrust again, and Taloka cried out when the knife plunged into his shoulder.

Taloka lowered the other shoulder and charged. Both went down. They rolled on the ground, and Michael lost his knife. He grabbed Taloka's knife hand, twisted the wrist, and the knife fell away. They rolled apart and struggled to their feet. They faced each other, gasping for breath, feet spread, circling, stumbling on the uneven ground.

Michael feinted with his left arm and landed a hard right to Taloka's belly. When Taloka bent forward from the blow, Michael landed a solid right to the head. Taloka crumpled and fell to the ground.

Michael gasped and leaned over Taloka. He lay motionless, face down. Michael dropped to his knees and felt around on the ground for his pistol. His hand found the barrel. He grasped the gun and stood, pushing the pistol under his belt.

Michael ran down the slope toward the fire, sliding on the spongy surface of needles and stumbling over loose stones and others that jutted from the ground. He slid the last few feet to the flat where the Indians had built their fire. The odor of burnt flesh made him momentarily dizzy. He felt his stomach churning. The warrior that he had shot lay across the fire pit, his flesh blackened where it touched the embers. Low flames licked each side of the body.

Michael grasped the man's ankles and pulled the body slowly from the fire. He dropped the legs abruptly at a thrashing sound beyond the dim circle of light from the fire. He jerked the pistol from his belt and pointed it toward the sound.

Maloskah emerged from the brushy cover. He held a knife at his side. Michael saw the blood on the blade.

"He's up there, unconscious. Taloka." Michael motioned up the hill with a nod of his head.

"Mmm! Mmm!" They both jumped at the muffled sound that came from the darkness. Michael pointed his pistol toward the sound. They saw the legs in the faint glow from the fire.

"Mmm, mmm, mmm," more urgently this time. They stepped into the gloom and saw Kimimela sitting on the ground, her hands and legs bound and tied to the tree she leaned against, a gag tied around her mouth. She stared wide-eyed at them. Maloskah worked on the knots on Kimimela's hands as Michael untied the gag and pulled it away.

"Ahhh," she said, gasping. "I thought I was dead."

Michael put his hands to her cheeks. "Are you okay?"

"Okay," she said. "How did you—" She gagged and choked. The tears came and rolled down her cheeks. Michael dropped to a knee beside her, put his arms around her and held her.

Maloskah dropped the leather thongs that had bound her hands. "I'll get Taloka," he said. He climbed up the slope and disappeared in the darkness.

Michael worked on the knots on Kimimela's legs. He pulled the thongs away and dropped them. He rubbed her leg gently where she had been bound.

"I was afraid," he said. He wanted to say more, to tell her that he was afraid that he had lost her, that he would never see her again, but he could not. She put her hand on his as he rubbed. She smiled weakly.

"Michael!" It was Maloskah, shouting from the hillside above. Michael and Kimimela started and looked above into the darkness.

"Where?" Maloskah shouted.

Michael ran up the slope, stumbling and sliding. He almost collided with Maloskah in the darkness. Michael looked at the ground and felt around with his feet and bent down to feel with his hands.

"Here. He was here," Michael said. But he was not there now.

They rode single-file at a walk in an aspen grove. The bright moon illuminated the white trunks of the aspen and cast shadows on the short grass, the trunks and shadows appearing as long parallel bars. They had not found Taloka's horses in the darkness, and they knew he was somewhere nearby, so they had not lingered.

Maloskah rode ahead, and Kimimela rode astride behind Michael. She held him around the waist and laid her head on his back. She fidgeted. She raised her head and spoke softly. "I don't like this saddle. I can't get close. You dress like a Beothuk. You talk like a Beothuk. You fight like a Beothuk. When are you going to ride like a Beothuk?"

He smiled. "That's hard. I'll work on it."

They rode in silence.

"Michael?"

"Yes?"

"We can paint your tipi," she said. He smiled, knowing she could not see it. He took her hand from his waist and kissed it. She replaced the hand at his waist and squeezed. She rested her head on his back.

The eastern horizon glowed with the promise of day. The pink tint at the bottom edge of a lacy cloud layer expanded and lightened as the sun ball appeared at the horizon and moved higher.

They rode through tall grasses on a faint hillside trail that descended gradually. Kimimela dozed, her arms locked around Michael's waist. They rounded a rocky outcropping and both riders stopped. Kimimela raised her head from Michael's back.

In the valley far below, they saw a sinuous line that at first glance resembled a long, thin snake. The snake materialized as a large army force. Hundreds of mounted troopers, a dozen small wheeled cannon and a long line of filled wagons at the rear.

"Bentley," Michael said. "He'll attack the village tomorrow. Two days early." He had spoken in English, more to himself than the others. Kimimela leaned toward Maloskah to interpret.

"I understand," Maloskah said. He whipped his horse and moved off rapidly at a gallop.

"Hold tight, Kimi," Michael said and kicked his horse into a gallop.

# CHAPTER TWENTY-ONE

### I Feel I'm Being Ripped Apart

Maloskah galloped into the village, followed closely by Michael. They reined in hard at the kiva, their lathered horses sliding to a stop. Michael and Kimimela slid off the horse together. Maloskah spoke to four warriors who had run over when they saw him coming. He told them to warn the villagers about the approach of the soldiers. The warriors ran toward the stream and their horses.

Maloskah rode down the lane below the kiva, shouting, "The wasichu army is coming! They will attack tonight or tomorrow! Get ready! Get ready!" He rode back and forth, shouting the warning. People came out of their tipis and gathered in the lane. They ran to their assigned posts and began preparations for the defense of the village.

Michael tied his horse's reins to the kiva hitching post. He stood quietly with Kimimela. They looked down the lane, watching the people scurry about, preparing for war.

"I thought we could prevent this," he said. They watched, their hope for peace and accommodation vanishing.

Kimimela turned to look up at him. "What will you do?"

He was quiet for a moment, staring down the lane. Then

he looked down at her. "Stay with you," he said. "If you will let me."

She took his hand, only a moment, then released it.

• • • •

Night. Defensive lines were manned by a few warriors, enough to sound the alarm if there should be a rare night attack. A brilliant moon cast shadows about the camp, dimly illuminating village structures and defenses.

Inside the kiva, a fire burned low in a pit at the center. A dozen elders and war leaders sat around the fire and stared into the flames. Their faces were colored an ethereal golden. At the back, against the wall of the circular kiva, Michael and Kimimela sat quietly. They watched the gathering at the fire.

The men at the fire circle were silent. They watched Howahkan hold a small bundle of sage over the flames. A thin spiral of gray smoke rose from the smoldering sage, spread and sparkled as the firelight played about the gray haze. Howahkan waved a feather to lightly brush the smoke over himself and the others. Then he sprinkled sprigs of sweetgrass on the embers. A sweet scent permeated the room.

Kimimela leaned toward Michael and whispered in his ear. "The sage drives the bad spirits away. Bad spirits hate sage. The sweetgrass purifies and calls the good spirits." Michael nodded. They looked back at the fire circle.

Howahkan slowly and methodically packed tobacco into a pipe. The stem of the pipe was of wood, the bowl of dark red stone. Twelve eagle feathers hung from the join between the stem and the bowl.

Howahkan held the pipe toward the man on his right.

This man leaned toward the fire and plucked a small ember from the fire with two green twigs. He touched the ember to the tobacco and held it there while Howahkan puffed. Howahkan held the stem of the pipe in his right hand and the bowl in his left. He puffed until the smoke swirled and curled about his head.

He pointed the mouthpiece to the four directions, then passed the pipe to the man on his left. This man took the pipe and held the pipe as had Howahkan. He put the pipe to his lips and smoked. He passed it to the man on his left, who did likewise. This was continued until all had smoked.

When the pipe had passed around the circle, it reached Howahkan once more. He turned the pipe upside down and tapped the bowl on a stone at the fire circle, dumping the ashes.

Without a word, the men stood and filed out. Howahkan was the last to leave.

Kimimela and Michael stood at the back. They watched the silent procession of tribal leaders, their heads lowered, each absorbed in his own thoughts.

Kimimela touched Michael's arm. "Michael, you go on," she said. "I must talk with Grandfather."

"What—"

"Please go. I will come later." She hurried to catch up with Howahkan.

Howahkan and Kimimela sat on each side of the fire pit in Howahkan's tipi. The new fire crackled, and the low flames flickered, rose and fell. The firelight cast dancing shadows on the tipi walls. They watched the flames, as if oblivious of the other's presence. Then Kimimela looked up at Howahkan and spoke softly.

"Grandfather, do you remember that I went on a vision

quest soon after my return from Mexico? I had been two years away from my village, and I wanted to remind myself who I was."

He nodded without looking at her.

"When I returned from the quest, I did not seek counsel, and I told you nothing had happened. Do you remember?"

Again, he nodded, still studying the flames.

"I did not tell the truth. What I saw made no sense to me. And it was disturbing. So I said nothing. May I tell you about it?"

Howahkan was silent a long moment, still peering into the fire. "What you did was wrong," he said. "You tried to interpret your own vision. It is not the Beothuk way."

"I know. I'm sorry. May I tell you now?"

"I am not a holy man. I will hear you only if you agree to seek counsel from a holy man if we do not understand your vision."

"Yes, I will do that," she said.

He looked up at her across the fire. "Tell me."

"I prepared for the quest as you and the elders had instructed me. I had fasted for four days before I focused on my vision.

"It was evening, and I was sitting on a large flat stone. Below me there was a clearing in the forest. I was weak and dizzy from hunger. I began to see images of four-legged and winged animals that ran and flew before me."

She rubbed her eyes with both hands and wiped beads of sweat from her temples.

"I saw Coyote. He trotted across the clearing. Then he saw me and stopped. He trotted back in front of me and sat on his haunches, looking at me. His eyes were piercing. I could feel them in my head.

"Dog trotted into the clearing. He saw Coyote and

growled. Then he saw me and stopped growling. He walked up stiff-legged beside Coyote, his tongue hanging from his mouth and saliva dripping. He sat on his haunches, looking at me. He relaxed, and his mouth closed. He almost seemed to smile.

"Then Wolf did the same thing. He snarled and started to attack Dog and Coyote. But when he saw me, he walked up beside them and sat on his haunches, looking at me. They all looked at me, right in my eyes."

Howahkan stared into the fire pit. The flames burned lower.

"Then the winged animals appeared. Magpie, Eagle, Hawk and Crow flew over the clearing and settled in the branches of the trees. Magpie and Crow made loud noises until they saw me. Then they were quiet. Other birds flew into the branches, and they all watched me.

"My head was spinning. I thought I would faint. I did not know what was happening.

"Then Butterfly flew into the clearing. She fluttered above Dog and Coyote and Wolf. Then she fluttered down before their faces. They stared at her as she flew slowly back and forth in front of them.

"She turned and flew toward me. She fluttered before my face, looking into my eyes. Then she settled on my shoulder, facing the animals. The animals looked at us, at me and at Butterfly. My head started spinning, and I passed out.

"When I woke up, I was lying on the ground. The animals were gone. I was very hungry, and I returned to the village."

Kimimela held her face in her hands. She looked up at Howahkan. She leaned toward him. "What does it mean, Grandfather?"

He stared into the dying fire. The flames flickered, and the red and orange embers glowed.

Kimimela watched him, waiting.

"You will not need to see the holy man," he said.

Kimimela still waited. "But what does it mean?"

He still stared into the flames. "Think, Kimimela. The animals."

She looked into the embers. She frowned and squeezed her eyes tightly shut. She rubbed her temples.

She sat up slowly. Her eyes opened wide. "No! . . . Impossible."

He looked at her. "Nothing is impossible, my child. You have had a powerful vision."

• • • •

A candle lantern on the desk softly illuminated the interior of Michael's tipi. He and Kimimela lay under the blanket. She was on her back. She stared into the darkness at the peak.

He watched her. He often tried to read her mood, but usually with no success. She remained a mystery to him. "Are you all right?" he said.

She turned to face him. She appeared to be in another place, frowning, her face drawn. Then she relaxed and smiled. She took his arm and pulled him to her.

"I'm glad Howahkan let you watch the pipe ceremony," she said. "It's very important to us. The sacred pipe was given to the Beothuk people by White Buffalo Calf Woman a long time ago. She told them that when a Beothuk smokes the sacred pipe, his voice goes to Kanta Kawan, the Great Spirit."

"Is this the same White Buffalo Calf Woman that is sacred to the Lakota?" Michael said.

"Yes," Kimimela said. "White Buffalo Calf Woman is sacred to the Beothuk, as she is to the Lakota. She taught the people how to pray and to sing sacred songs. She said she would come again someday, and the Beothuk people would be saved from whatever threatened them."

"Do all Beothuk people believe this?" Michael said.

"Yes."

"Do you?" he said.

She pulled the blanket to her chin. She pondered. "I told the Sisters in Mexico City about White Buffalo Calf Woman. They became very excited. They said I was blessed. They said that White Buffalo Calf Woman was the Virgin Mary."

"Did they, by God!" Michael said. He stifled a laugh.

"I told the Baptist teachers at the American school about White Buffalo Calf Woman and what the Sisters had said. They said it was heresy and nonsense. I told them it was no more nonsense than their Jesus story. They were very angry with me. They wanted to make me leave the school, but—"

"The school wanted your grandfather's gold," Michael said.

She laughed. "Yes."

Michael pulled her to him and kissed her on her mouth, her nose, her eyes. He gently caressed her breasts through the blanket. She grasped both of his hands in hers and held them.

"Now, I don't know what I believe," she said. "I am in two worlds and part of neither one. I want to believe the old ways, the Beothuk ways, but I have seen so much of other ways that I think I don't believe anything spiritual."

He put his arms around her and held her. She snuggled against him, feeling warm and secure in his arms.

First light. The eastern horizon glowed, though the sun disk had not yet appeared. Gray shapes began to emerge from the darkness. Behind a low ridge, a large mounted cavalry troop in a column of fours stood in good order. Horses fidgeted, shifted their weight, moved about, and troopers pulled their mounts back into line. The only sounds were the creak of leather and clink of metal fittings.

On the other side of the ridge, dismounted troopers lay in a long line behind the protection of a low embankment. They looked across a field of knee-high grass at the main village of The People. The grass rippled and whispered in the soft dawn.

Most of the troopers held repeating rifles that rested on the embankment. Some crouched beside the tubular shoulder-held weapons that lay on the ground at their feet. At intervals in the line of riflemen, small cannon were positioned. Behind these lines, small mortars were in place with projectiles stacked alongside.

••••

In the village, warriors crouched and lay behind built earthen embankments. They held rifles and tubular shoulder weapons. Others sat beside mortars, arranging and rearranging the stacks of projectiles. Some women were among the warriors.

There were also visitors among the defenders. Howahkan had sent messengers to Beothuk villages and to tribes, members of the confederation, near and distant. Groups of warriors from nearby Beothuk and Lakota villages had already arrived. A party of fifty Cheyenne rode in the previous day. They had been hunting two days' ride away and had been alerted by one of Howahkan's riders.

Some old people, children and women stood beside the

kiva, close enough to the entrance that they could hurry inside, if necessary. They looked around anxiously. The silence and the waiting were oppressive. The rich, gurgling, descending warble of a near meadowlark was amplified in the stillness. Another answered from a distance.

Kimimela and Michael stood in the open near the kiva entrance. Kimimela looked at Michael. His face was contorted, as if in pain. It was a face that she had not seen before. She took his hand in hers.

He turned to her. "I feel like I'm being ripped apart," he said. She took his arm with both hands and pulled him close.

# CHAPTER TWENTY-TWO

## It Is Finished

Major Bentley and Captain Jackson sat their horses quietly on the flat crest of the hillock that overlooked the army position. A guard of twenty mounted troopers sat their horses quietly nearby. Sergeant Clark held his mount in check at the head of the guard.

The commander studied his position, his force and his prospect.

"Are we ready?" Bentley said.

"Yes, sir," Jackson said. Major Bentley looked below.

"Well, then. Proceed."

"Yes, sir!" Captain Jackson said. He saluted smartly. Major Bentley casually returned the salute.

Captain Jackson whirled his horse and galloped down off the hillock toward a command post behind the cannons and mortars. The officers below saw him coming and gathered at the post.

Jackson reined in sharply. He dismounted and handed his reins to an orderly. The officers huddled around him. After a minute of huddled conversation, the group broke apart, and officers strode off to their posts.

One of the officers shouted a command. Immediately a barrage from the army cannon and mortars opened. Shock waves, smoke and explosions rose from the army lines. The cannon fire was followed by the *whumpf* of mortars and rifle fire from the troopers who kneeled and lay behind embankments.

The army barrage was answered by mortar and rifle fire from the village. The battle was joined.

Warriors crouched behind earthen embankments. Shots from the army line struck the embankments with a dull thump. Some shots zipped overhead and struck tipis or the kiva wall.

Mortar tenders dropped missiles into the muzzles of their small cannon and covered their ears as the missiles were launched toward the army lines. Warriors holding shoulder weapons rose behind the embankment and sent their charges streaking toward the army position.

Along the line, defenders were struck and fell where they lay until taken away by women and old men.

The troopers behind their embankment fired at will at the Beothuk lines. The firing was sporadic and unhurried. When a trooper's magazine was empty, he slid down the incline and reloaded casually.

The growing sounds of the battle rose to a crescendo that materialized as a pounding of hooves. Troopers looked to their left to see a mounted force bearing down on them. A hundred mounted warriors led by Taloka galloped straight toward the left flank of the army line. The warriors brandished spears and rifles, firing as they charged.

All soldiers in the line turned their rifles and fired on the charging warriors. Most of the riders died in the first volley. They fell from their mounts before reaching the army position. The bodies tumbled, and the horses veered off and scattered.

Only Taloka and ten others reached the army line and broke through. Soldiers rose from their positions and swarmed about the terrified horses. The troopers pulled the warriors from their mounts and encircled them. The outnumbered Beothuk fought hand-to-hand with the soldiers, knives and spears against sabers and pistols.

Olaktay and Taloka stood side by side, fighting a dozen troopers who fired on them with rifles and pistols. Olaktay, a bloody circle enlarging on his chest, turned to Taloka. Olaktay's mouth hung open, and he stared at Taloka in disbelief. A soldier plunged a saber into Olaktay's chest, and he fell.

Taloka looked around frantically. His followers lay scattered about on the ground, all dead. He was alone. Four soldiers stood before him, two with rifles and two with sabers. Taloka dropped his knife and looked up at the heavens. He had voiced but the first note of his death song when the two soldiers plunged their sabers into his chest. He fell to his knees. The soldiers pulled their sabers from his chest, and his dead body fell forward.

Most of the people who had stood near the kiva before the battle commenced had retreated inside. Only Michael and Kimimela stood at the entrance, watching the battle. A child, a little girl of three years, walked up beside Kimimela and peered outside. Kimimela pushed her back inside.

As they watched, an army cavalry force broke through the warrior defense. Brandishing sabers and firing pistols, troopers rode over the earthen barrier. Some warriors were trampled by the charging horses. Others pulled back, fighting hand to hand as soldiers struck with their sabers. Kimimela gasped when a running warrior was shot down almost at her feet.

Michael and Kimimela watched a mounted trooper chase a woman who ran across the open space between the embankment and the kiva. She carried a rifle but could not use it as she ran.

"Ina!" They had not seen the three-year-old run out of the kiva. She darted from the entrance and ran toward her mother.

The mother dropped her rifle and ran for the child. The mounted trooper raised his saber to strike.

Michael bent over the downed warrior at his feet, seized his rifle, pointed toward the charging trooper and fired. The soldier's horse was thrown sideways when it was hit, and the trooper fell from the saddle. He scrambled up and ran toward the army lines. A mounted trooper rode alongside and hoisted him up behind him.

The mother scooped up the child and ran inside the kiva.

"Michael!" Kimimela shouted. He looked up to see a mounted trooper charging him, his saber raised to strike. Michael grasped the rifle in both hands and readied it to ward off the trooper's saber.

What happened next was a blur. The charging trooper, with saber raised, leaned toward Michael to strike him. At the same time, Michael raised the rifle over his head to block the saber chop.

They froze in time.

It was Lieutenant Worth. The lieutenant lowered his saber, and Michael lowered the rifle. Worth reined his horse hard leftward, spun around and galloped toward the army lines. He jumped the Beothuk earthen embankment and was gone.

Michael dropped the rifle. He stared open-mouthed toward the army lines and saw nothing through the tears and sweat that ran into his eyes. He shook his head and tried to focus.

Troopers and warriors fought hand to hand at the embankment. Those troopers still mounted wheeled their horses and galloped for the army lines. Some slowed beside unhorsed comrades and pulled them up behind their saddles. Other unhorsed soldiers on foot ran toward the army position.

Michael watched the soldiers gallop and run for their lines. *God be with them,* he thought. When the soldiers were safe behind their fortification, firing intensified. Nothing had been gained, nothing lost.

Michael turned to face Kimimela. She hardly recognized him. He had become another person, marked by pain and loss. His arms hung limply at his side. She walked to him and took his arm. She held him close and hoped that his spirit would survive with his body.

Thirty mounted warriors sat their horses quietly in a copse on a slope a mile above the village. Most horsemen carried rifles. Some held spears. The horses shifted from side to side and were reined in by their riders. Howahkan and Maloskah sat their horses a bit to the side. They talked softly.

Howahkan looked at the warriors. All looked directly at him, waiting. He nodded to Maloskah. Howahkan walked his horse a few steps, then kicked his mount into a gallop. Maloskah and the warriors charged after him. The riders spread and plunged down the slope, slanting leftward from the village and battleground.

Major Bentley and Sergeant Clark stood at the edge of the hillock, watching the action below. A soldier standing nearby held the reins of their mounts. The major's guard of mounted troopers milled about behind them.

The soldiers in the guard heard the muffled sound of hooves below, but they saw nothing. The sounds increased, and Howahkan's force exploded over the edge of the hillock, charging up the slope. The warriors fired their rifles as they came. The soldiers frantically pulled rifles from boots and attempted to return fire as their horses shied at the sudden appearance of mounted warriors charging straight for them.

Howahkan, at the head of the charge, was hit immediately on reaching the flat at the top of the hillock. He fell heavily from the saddle, and the warriors swerved to avoid trampling the tumbling body.

The warriors encircled the soldiers and killed most of them with rifle fire, clubs and spears. Major Bentley and Sergeant Clark had run for their horses at the first glimpse of the charging warriors. Clark was speared in the back before he could mount. Major Bentley had just swung up into his saddle when his horse was shot out from under him. He rolled from the saddle and scrambled up. He pulled his pistol from its holster and looked around desperately for help.

Major Bentley was alone. He aimed his pistol at a warrior. Before Bentley could fire, two mounted warriors fired on him with their rifles, and a third urged his horse forward and thrust his spear in his chest. Bentley toppled backward, dead.

Maloskah and another warrior slid off their horses and ran to Howahkan's body. They lifted it and draped it across Maloskah's horse. Maloskah mounted and led the warriors in a galloping withdrawal down the hillock.

It was eerily quiet. Firing had ceased. Warriors were at their positions behind earthworks and hillocks. Waiting, looking.

A meadowlark called in the distance, its flute-like song piercing. The peculiar smell of war was the only evidence that a battle had been fought. Until one glanced around at the carnage. Some who were whole tended to the wounded. Others carried off the dead.

Maloskah and his warriors rode slowly into the village. They stopped at the kiva entrance and dismounted. The people stood silent and watched Maloskah and the others gently lift the body of Howahkan from the horse and lower it to the ground. Kimimela dropped to her knees beside the body.

Warriors at the defensive line stood and watched. They were exposed and easy targets, but they were oblivious to any danger.

Then, as if on signal, those on the defensive positions turned and faced the army lines.

• • • •

A soldier, on foot, led a horse that carried the body of Major Bentley draped across the saddle. A dozen soldiers on foot followed. Riflemen and cannoneers stood at their positions and watched the procession. The group stopped in front of Captain Jackson. Jackson stiffened. It struck him only at that moment. He realized that he was in command.

"Set him down," Captain Jackson said. The soldier who had brought him in lifted the body from the saddle and gently lowered it to the ground. Troopers all along the line stood silent, watching, aware but oblivious that they were in the open and easy targets.

When the body was at rest on the ground, the soldiers turned, as if on signal, and stared at the village. They saw the warriors who stood behind their embankment, watching the soldiers.

The combatants, enemies, stared at each other across the meadow, trampled and wearing the bodies of soldiers and warriors alike.

Warriors and soldiers, behind their lines, turned away from the field. Soldiers walked toward their mounts and wagons, warriors toward their village. It was finished.

The round crest of the setting sun disappeared, leaving thin layers of lacy clouds from horizon to horizon, colored with a multitude of shades of orange and vermillion and purple and pink.

Michael rode bareback at full gallop along the edge of a bare plateau. He wore fringed Beothuk clothing, his hair blowing wildly about his head, a single feather in his hair.

On a ledge below, Kimimela rode bareback at a gallop in the same direction. Her long braids streamed out behind her, flying above her horse's long outstretched tail. She drummed the horse's sides with her heels.

At a slash in the hillside, Kimimela turned her horse upward, drumming with her heels and lashing the horse's flanks with her quirt. The horse charged up the cut toward the top of the plateau.

She reached the top of the cut just as Michael passed. He did not slow, and she drummed her horse hard with her heels and pulled up beside him.

They galloped on, eyes ahead, taking no apparent notice of each other. They lashed with quirts, as if they were about to take flight.

Finally, they slowed and pulled their mounts to a sliding stop. Kimimela slid off her mount. Michael threw a leg over and slid off.

They stood by their heaving mounts, close, but not touching. Looking, searching. What to do, what to say, sadness written on their faces.

She reached for him, and their arms intertwined. He pulled her to him and held her close, burying his face in her hair. He leaned back to look into her face, then slowly pulled her to him again and rested his head on hers.

# CHAPTER TWENTY-THREE

A Convocation of Two Great Peoples

A meadow in a broad valley, roughly equidistant between the main village of The People and Fort Andrew Jackson. On this September day, the short grass had lost its lush green color, tending now toward a dry, golden hue. Scattered deciduous trees were just beginning to show a hint of autumn color.

The newly constructed large arbor of logs looked alien in the otherwise pristine landscape. A loose covering of hand-hewn planks provided a patchy shade.

The multitude of Americans, most dressed in stark black suits and starched white shirts, stood near the arbor. They looked distinctly out of place. They smoked their cigars and talked animatedly, gesturing and laughing.

Two dozen Beothuk men, wearing their finest skin clothing and accessories and feathers, stood quietly in a cluster on the other side of the arbor. Warriors from other tribes, dressed in distinctive clothing, stood about in groups, sometimes mingling with members of other tribes, once enemies, now confederates. There were delegations of Cheyenne, Lakota, Crow, Blackfoot, Kiowa, Ute and Arapaho, and others.

There were also representatives from more distant tribes that were contemplating joining the confederation: Navajo, Comanche, Shoshone, Paiute, Modoc, Klamath and Nez Perce.

Four Americans wearing serious black suits and ties sat under the arbor at a round table made of fresh green planks. A short, rotund gentleman apparently was the principal Washington representative, judging from the deference paid him by the others. Major Burke and Captain Jackson sat on the right side of the black suits.

Behind the Americans, a mixed gathering of farmers, lawyers, merchants, a few soldiers and curious idlers stood. They peered over shoulders and jockeyed for a better look.

Opposite the government black suits, Maloskah, Kimimela and two Americans in black suits sat at the table. Behind these, a considerable number of Indians stood. They represented the tribes that were most instrumental in the origins and operation of the confederation.

On the table before each of the delegations, there was a ceramic inkwell and two quills.

Between the two groups of delegates sat a distinguished-looking American gentleman in a black suit as severe as his countenance. He looked at the Indians, smiled thinly as if the effort was something new to him, and then at the American delegation.

Severe Black Suit pushed his spectacles up on his nose and picked up a paper from the table. He read: "We are here today as representatives of two great peoples to discuss two historic propositions."

Kimimela bent toward Maloskah and whispered in his ear. He nodded.

"The first proposition has two parts: To wit: (1) That each side recognizes the sovereignty of the other side. (2)

That there shall be a division of territory at the hundredth Meridian, which Meridian shall run from the border with Upper Canada southward to the boundary of the Republic of Texas. It is understood that this proposition shall be speedily agreed to today by both sides."

Severe Black Suit lowered the document and looked at both delegations, as if to give them time to digest the reading, or to give him time to get his breath.

During the reading, Kimimela had occasionally whispered in Maloskah's ear until he raised his hand to silence her. She had not whispered to him again.

Severe Black Suit raised the document and resumed reading: "As to the second proposition: To wit: That there shall be a confederation of the two great nations that shall be termed the United Nations of America. It is understood that this proposition shall be considered by each side and settled at another convocation at this same place three months from this date."

Severe Black Suit leaned back and looked at each delegation, as if to invite questions or comments, though he had no intention of entertaining discussion.

He returned to the document and continued: "It is further agreed that The People will begin discussions immediately with the Republic of Texas and the Republic of Mexico for the purpose of defining boundaries between those republics and the sovereign territory of The People."

Severe Black Suit lowered the document and looked around the table, as if to ensure that all were paying proper attention. He inhaled deeply and read: "And, finally, that both parties hereby agree that they will have no further intercourse whatsoever with the foreign element called the Celestials."

Severe Black Suit looked around the table, smiled benignly and, seeing no visible reaction, appeared to collapse in his chair.

He recovered and tendered the document to Maloskah. Maloskah took the paper and leaned toward Kimimela. She spoke softly to him.

Maloskah picked up a quill from the table and dipped it in the inkwell. Slowly and methodically, he signed his name in block letters: "MALOSKAH." He replaced the quill on the table and glanced at Kimimela. She smiled.

Maloskah slid the document and inkwell to Kimimela. She picked up a quill, dipped it into the inkwell and signed her name with a flourish. She picked up the document, blew on the signature to dry it, and handed it to Severe Black Suit. He frowned and took the paper with his thumb and forefinger, as if it had suddenly become contaminated.

Kimimela smiled at him. He raised an eyebrow.

Severe Black Suit passed the paper to the Washington representative.

This gentleman thrust out his right arm stiffly to adjust his coat sleeve, picked up the quill from the table and dipped it into the inkwell. He signed with a great abundance of slashes and curlicues and replaced the quill on the table. He picked up the paper, leaned forward and offered it to Severe Black Suit, who took it with a nod of his head.

The Washington representative and Maloskah stood simultaneously. Kimimela rose slowly. The Washington gentleman briskly offered his hand to Maloskah, and they shook hands.

Kimimela extended her hand toward the Washington representative. She smiled. He hadn't expected this and wasn't sure how to react. After a slight hesitation, he leaned across the table and took her hand. When they touched, he smiled and shook her hand. She released his hand and turned away.

The convocation had ended. The Americans seated at the table stood, turned and chatted with others around them.

Kimimela leaned toward Maloskah and said something in his ear. They turned toward the group who stood behind them. Maloskah walked to the group and spoke to a man standing in the front row. The two of them walked from the arbor, talking.

Kimimela glanced at a knot of black suits standing and chatting outside the arbor. They formed a tight circle, pontificating, laughing and chatting loudly. Except one.

John Wesley Throckmorton was looking straight at her. He smiled timidly. She walked toward him. He stepped away from the group toward her.

"We received your letter," she said soberly. His smile vanished, and he looked at her with apprehension.

"You are welcome," she said, smiling. He exhaled and smiled broadly. "Very welcome," she said. Kimimela looked over his shoulder. John Wesley turned around and followed her gaze.

There stood Walika, her hands on her cheeks. She looked directly at John Wesley.

He walked slowly to her. She looked up at him, her hands still on her cheeks. He put his arms around her shoulders and held her tightly. She laid her head on his chest, her arms hanging at her sides, tears streaming down her cheeks. She raised her head abruptly and looked around, suddenly terrified. She stepped back and smiled timidly.

Walika and John Wesley walked away, side by side, not touching.

Kimimela smiled. She walked back to the Indian spectators who stood behind the conference table. She spoke to a handsomely dressed Cheyenne.

The Washington delegates strolled chatting from the arbor in twos and threes. One of the delegates remained standing at the table with Major Burke. He pulled a cigar from a breast pocket and offered it to Burke. Burke declined with a shake of his head and a smile.

The delegate put the cigar in his mouth, lit it and pulled deeply on it. He exhaled contentedly, eyes closed, smoke billowing around the heads of the two.

The delegate removed the cigar from his mouth. "That went very well," he said. Smoke streamed from his mouth and his nostrils. "I think this affair will be settled amicably."

He leaned toward Burke and spoke animatedly. "Now, do you think we can arrange that buffalo shoot?"

Major Burke smiled. "It's all set. You'll be guided ably by one of our new confederates."

"Splendid!" The representative smiled broadly. He did a little shuffling jig.

He stopped and turned serious. "By the way," the delegate said, "I heard a curious story about an army officer who went to The People as an ambassador of sorts. An interesting story. If true."

"Yes," said Burke, "quite true."

The representative was surprised. "Really? What happened to him?"

Major Burke frowned. He lowered his head, then looked up. "Sad story. He was killed in action. A brave fellow. Died for his country."

"Hmm. Yes. A sad story indeed." The representative pondered with a grim face.

Then he brightened. He smiled broadly, waved his cigar and turned to leave. "Until tomorrow! Oh, I am looking forward to this shoot!" He clapped Burke on the back and strutted away, his shoulders thrown back, smoke seeming to stream from his ears.

Burke remained. He looked across the table at the group of Beothuk who chatted softly. Kimimela faced the group, her back to the table. She moved a step to the side, revealing the face of Michael who stood in the second line of spectators. He was fully dressed in Indian garb, with a single feather hanging from his hair.

Michael looked directly at Major Burke. They made eye contact. The slightest hint of a smile played about Burke's lips.

# EPILOGUE

A dozen mounted Washington black suits rode on a well-worn trail behind their army escort of thirty soldiers. Two black suits rode apart from the others.

"The worst part of the affair was our promise not to deal with the Celestials," one said. "Their stuff would have been of great value to us in this country and abroad. Too bad."

His companion smiled and leaned toward him. "Hah!" he said. "I will tell you in strictest confidence, my good man. As we speak, Mr. Colt and his associates have all of the Celestial armaments in hand and will have improved models in production in short order."

He faced forward and spoke softly.

"And then we shall see."

# AFTERWORD

This is a work of fiction, an alternate history with science fiction elements. I have taken outrageous liberties with time and place, altering either or both when necessary to suit the story line. For this reason, I have not mentioned dates or identified places in the narrative.

I did not wish to offend any particular tribe with my curious story, so I have crafted my tale around a tribe that was living in Newfoundland at the time of the early contacts with Europeans in the late fifteenth century, though the Beothuk or ancestors of the Beothuk clashed with the Norse as early as the year 1000 A.D. The tribe was declared officially extinct when the last full-blood Beothuk died in 1829. Or did they withdraw westward from contact with whites and settle eventually in the western plains?

# A LOOK AT: THIS NEW COUNTRY: A WESTERN DOUBLE

**2017 WILL ROGERS MEDALLION AWARD WINNER**

Unable to come to terms with a family tragedy in Virginia, Caleb drifts westward, seeking anonymity or death. He fears nothing, since he has already lost everything. He learns to fight and kill and is untouched by the result. For Caleb, there is no retribution, no penalty, no tomorrow, only today.

Soon after he begins gold dredging in the Stanley Basin in central Idaho, he rescues Mei Lin, a young Chinese prostitute, from a brothel and promises to find a place for her. Caleb has found a new purpose in his life – he begins to hope and to care, and Mei Lin is at the center of the change. But does he dare tell her of his love and invite her into his uncertain life?

Each scarred by personal tragedy, Caleb and Mei Lin develop a love stronger than ever on their journey to the New West.

This New Country includes: A Place for Mei Lin and Home to Wyoming.

*AVAILABLE NOW*

# ABOUT THE AUTHOR

Harlan Hague traveled a circuitous road to western literature. A native Texan, he earned business degrees at Baylor University and University of Texas and worked in management for four years before receiving his enlightenment and switching career and field to teaching history. He earned a further two degrees, the last a Ph.D. in history from University of Nevada, Reno. He taught United States history, American West and the environment at San Joaquin Delta College and summers at Cal State Stanislaus and University of Oregon.

While teaching, Hague wrote a few dozen history articles on the American West that published in scholarly journals. He turned to writing books and, in the process, received a number of academic and professional honors and grants, including National Endowment for the Humanities.

Since turning to books, Harlan Hague writes about people searching for redemption and fulfillment in the West, running from their demons, leaning on others. He likes endings that close with a sigh and a question. His books have won several awards in national competitions. His screenplays, mostly based on his books, have earned some notice and are making the rounds.